I WAS SHIPWRECKED

ON THE

Andrea Doria!

To Terry

Pierette Simpson

5-2-13

I WAS SHIPWRECKED

ON THE

Andrea Doria!

— THE TITANIC OF THE 1950s —

PIERETTE DOMENICA SIMPSON

BRIQ
Publications, LLC

Copyright © 2012 Pierette Domenica Simpson
Cover and interior design by Ted Ruybal

ISBN 13: 978-0-9850776-0-0
LCCN: 2012931871
First Edition
1 2 3 4 5 6 7 8 9 10

FIC002000 FICTION / Action & Adventure

Publications, LLC

For information, please contact:
P.O. Box 846
Novi, Michigan 48376
Pierette@PieretteSimpson.com
www.IWasShipwreckedontheAndreaDoria.com

Educators will find curriculum ideas on our site.

Cover: The *Stockholm* ramming the *Andrea Doria's* starboard side.
(Courtesy of Maurizio Eliseo)

Dedication

To my grandparents, who raised me with love and
sacrificed all of their worldly goods and ways
to accompany me to America.

To my mother, who welcomed me to the New World.

To all of the *Andrea Doria* rescuers: Captain Calamai
and his crew, rescue ships and their seamen,
and services of the Red Cross.

To my fellow passengers on the *Andrea Doria,*
with whom I share a special bond.

Remembering 100 Years

In honor of those who sailed on the *Titanic,* the *Andrea Doria,* and the *Costa Concordia.*

May your courage and sacrifice inspire us all to confront the mighty forces of the sea with intelligence, compassion, and bravery.

Prologue

— July 26, 1956 —

"Don't jump!" we heard the crewman beg from above. "Wait your turn for the rope! Everybody, wait your turn!"

Is Patrick going to listen to an adult for the first time? I wondered in suspense.

I watched my ship buddy lower his leg from the metal railing. Those of us already in the lifeboat understood Patrick's dilemma: Should a nine-year-old take his chances at survival by plunging into the black, shark-infested waters and swimming to the lifeboat? Or should he wait his turn behind other desperate passengers waiting to take lives into their own hands—literally—by grabbing the rope and slowly descending several stories?

Patrick was holding his mother and his older sister, Darlene, away from the railing, as if in command of the situation. Before my grandparents and I had abandoned the listing vessel, Patrick had been encouraging his family to jump, telling them, "I know the ship's gonna sink. We have to jump now!" Was he now willing to obey orders for the first time on this ten-day voyage?

We saw dozens of passengers taking deliberate steps toward the only rope down to the ocean. *Come on, come on!* I cheered them on in my mind.

They seemed patient, perhaps because there was nowhere else to go. But once it was their turn to hurl their bodies over the railing, reach for the rope, and lower themselves, they became more agitated. Some screamed and refused to do it. Others cursed those who froze in panic halfway to the lifeboat. "Let go! Keep moving! If you don't keep moving, I'll come and step on your hands!" Some of them did just that; their victims fell into our bobbing vessel with a thud.

My buddy Patrick took to the rope with the ease of an ape in his native jungle. As his sister and his mother and the rest of us watched, Patrick showed off his boldness. Wearing his orange life vest, he flung his body over the railing, grabbed the rope, and began to swing—as far from the sinking vessel as his strength would allow him.

"What's that crazy kid doing?" someone yelled from the lifeboat. I watched nervously (and in secret admiration) as Patrick's little body whirled in circles above our heads. *Patrick is up to his daredevil self,* I thought. *He's enjoying one more adventure on the high seas.*

Suddenly, after a few moments of comic relief, my heart stopped, as a collective gasp rose from my fellow survivors. Patrick's luck was being challenged. Halfway through one of his swings, his life vest got stuck on a hook sticking out from the side of the ship, and the rope was swinging by itself.

I looked at my grandparents; they were making the sign of the cross. They looked more scared than when they'd been desperately making their own way down to the lifeboat on the rope, my grandma holding her purse, my grandpa with his briefcase in one hand.

How can Patrick get unstuck? I asked myself.

I held my breath. My friend's arms and legs flailed as he fumbled fiercely to grab the back of his life vest. He reminded me of a freshly hooked fish frantically flipping its body with all its might in a fight for freedom. Except that Patrick didn't seem truly frantic—just busy.

"Look at that old man running down to the next deck! Maybe he's headed for Patrick!" a young woman in the lifeboat hollered.

The old man reached Patrick, unhooked the life vest, and gave the boy a push toward the swinging rope. Patrick caught it in midair and made a swift descent. He landed with a thump— and a smile on his face! His mother and sister, who had been watching all of this while waiting in line, hugged each other and cried.

They're so happy! Thank God! I was relieved for my friends.

No one dared to say anything except for the French crewman who had rowed from the rescue ship. "You're lucky to be alive, *mon ami!*"

A woman exclaimed, "We're all safe now!"

"You're not safe yet, Madame," the Frenchman said, pointing to the giant funnel almost parallel to the ocean, hovering over our heads, ready to capsize the luxury liner *Andrea Doria.*

Others scrambled to climb down, including Patrick's family. I waited to see Darlene's reaction toward her brother. She simply hugged him, as did his mother. None of us felt very expressive; we were mostly just vomiting as the swell of each wave drove us upward, smashed into the hull of the ship, and swooped back down.

"Lower your heads so I don't hit you with the oars," the crewman warned us. He looked exhausted as he rowed a packed lifeboat back to his French liner.

Patrick refused to duck. I heard him say to his mother, "I don't wanna smell all this vomit!" He wasn't going near the floor of the bobbing vessel.

I retched and retched. I was a nine-year-old girl who had been swallowing fear and trauma for hours. I was too tired to think about how, just hours earlier, my family had been heading from our home in Italy toward the promised land of America. All I could think was, *Is everyone going to get off the ship and make it home?*

A Sad Good-bye to Pranzalito

— *Tuesday, July 17, 1956* —

Piera

This is the saddest day of my nine and a half years, I thought as I looked around our gravel courtyard filled with friends. My grandparents and I had, for years, prepared for this upheaval. But that didn't ease our sadness on this final day in our homeland. Even holding tickets for America, the Promised Land, couldn't cure the melancholy that shrouded my family and my village of Pranzalito on this day.

For a week, we had been receiving visits from most of the 120 people in our town—a place blessed with forests, rivers, and fertile farmland nestled at the foot of the Italian Alps. Everyone understood that today was reserved for close family and friends to say their good-byes. My friends Domenica, Gianni, Roberto, and Assunta all came to hug me. "*Mi mancherai!*" whispered my best friend, Domenica, telling me with tears in her eyes that she would miss me. I told them all that I would miss them, too, that I would return, and that we would play together again.

I felt special when my godmother, Isa, pulled her car into the courtyard. She had driven for an hour from the big city of Torino to see me off. I hugged her and kissed her really hard on both cheeks, the way Italians do to show affection.

She told me to stay a good girl and have a very safe trip: "*Stai brava, Piera. Ti auguro un viaggio molto salvo!*" I knew that I would miss her voice, her visits, gifts of chocolate, and tender caresses on my face. It crossed my mind that this was the second time she'd said an important good-bye to my family. I had seen a picture of her holding me, an eighteen-month-old, while my mother, teary-eyed, left us for America. *Today, we're making almost the same picture,* I thought.

My grandparents—my dear Nonnis, as I called them—faced their pain more directly than I did. Nonno, a robust farmer, could not hold back a flood of tears; he circled the courtyard wiping his eyes. Nonna, a strong woman in spite of her delicate features, was more dramatic than Nonno. "People our age shouldn't leave their home, family, and farm—unless they're crazy!" she kept saying. I think she enjoyed being the center of attention. I know that she was genuinely mourning the passing of the only life that she and her husband had ever known, the only friends, the only family, the only land. She was leaving behind her mother, two sisters, aunts and uncles, and cousins.

My loving Nonnis had decided to make the ultimate sacrifice for me. They would accompany me to Detroit, Michigan, where I would "meet" my mother and become a member of the family she had started there.

Our dear friend Giuseppe was anxious to drive us to the seaport of Genoa, where our four trunks had been loaded aboard the luxurious passenger liner *Andrea Doria*. The ship was known for transporting many immigrants seeking the American Dream. We were confident that it would give safe passage to family belongings, my First Communion dress, Persian rugs, handmade blankets, and stylish Italian sweaters on a transatlantic crossing.

"You'd better get in the car," Giuseppe instructed. "You don't want to miss the boat." His teasing was meant to help lighten our mood.

Nonno gestured for Nonna and Nonna Apollonia, my sweet great-grandmother, to get into the black sedan. It was a great comfort having Nonna Apollonia, the strongest bond to our motherland, accompany us.

But my closest pals were not coming along. I ran to my loving farm dog Titti and my "baby" cat Carla, my playmates when my friends weren't around. I hadn't been crying yet, but now the tears couldn't help flowing. I sobbed. It was all sinking in.

Nonna pulled me away from my pals and led me by hand to the car. *"Non piangere, Piera."* She asked me not to cry, but I could tell by the tone of her voice that she knew I couldn't help it. We all cried.

As the car wound its way out of the courtyard, entered the dirt road, and traveled past the twelve-foot-tall corn stalks, I thought about all the places I would miss in Pranzalito: the one-room schoolhouse where I had finished third grade, the river Chiusella which irrigated our fields, the church at the top of a hill where we prayed, and the Tabacchiaio-Bar, the store, bar, tobacconist, and general gathering place where you could watch the only TV in town and play bocce ball. *Where will Nonno show off his bocce ball skills in Detroit? Where will I go to church with Nonna, and what will my new school be like? How soon before I will see these familiar places again?*

The car ride seemed long. My body was sleepy, but my mind was excited. I wanted to stay awake to get the first glimpse of our ship, but Nonna was scaring me a little. She kept telling Nonna Apollonia how awful it was to make people float on water for ten days just to get to America. I heard her whisper, "But Piera didn't want to fly. She decided that airplanes are too dangerous." I was glad not to be flying, but I didn't like hearing about the dangers of water travel. *She's an old grown-up,* I thought. *She's supposed to be able to handle this.*

I remembered my godmother being concerned about the

river Chiusella flooding. Just a few hours ago in our courtyard, she had whispered to a group of villagers about a nightmare she'd had: "The buildings collapsed, and everyone fell in the water. Piera's mother swam a long way to reach her."

Nightmares are strange, I thought as I finally fell asleep, exhausted by the day's emotions.

From a deep slumber, I awoke to tender nudges from my two Nonnas. "Is this the port? Where is the *Andrea Doria?* Is it boarding time?" I thought this was going to be the most exciting day of my life, so I wanted to know about everything I would be doing—right then and there! But because I was in a hurry, it all seemed to be moving in slow motion.

Nonna Apollonia kept pecking at my cheeks and forehead while squeezing me against her rotund body. *I hope she lets me go soon. We've got to board. Oh, she's crying really hard now.*

I had wondered at first why she couldn't come with us, but, as I said now to make her feel better, "Nonna, you have to stay and feed Titti and Carla for me. We'll be back!" These excuses seemed reasonable, even though I knew I had made them up.

"*Ti voglio bene, Piera!*" she said softly. She was always telling me that she loved me, especially when I visited her a few houses down the road. And she would sweeten the words with a piece of creamy dark chocolate.

At this moment, I felt torn between savoring her sweetness and moving toward my new destination. I gave her a quick squeeze and said, *"Ti voglio bene."* It was bittersweet.

Nonno gave a manly hug to Giuseppe, grabbed his brown briefcase, checked on the clasp, and took me by the hand. Being between my Nonnis gave me a sense of security. We pushed through a crowd of tearful, confused-looking people. *Are they immigrants like us?* I wondered.

After what seemed like an eternity, I looked up and saw a huge white structure. "The *Andrea Doria!*" I announced.

"Si, Cici." Nonna always called me by that nickname for little girls, but now it didn't sound right. I wanted to be called Piera.

The gangplank lay in front of us, and it meant walking over water. *Will Nonna do it without screaming?* I tugged on her arm so hard that she had to move forward without second thoughts.

Soon we had boarded the ship that everyone in Pranzalito had been talking about. The modern, safe, and beautiful ship that made Italy proud! I couldn't wait to see why she was called a floating art museum. I felt lucky to meet her.

After a warm welcome by two crewmen, we made our way to the main deck. The Genoese sun was drenching us with warm wishes, as it drenched the rolling hills of Genoa. It made my Nonnis rediscover their smiles. We joined other passengers in waving white handkerchiefs. *"Arrivederci!"* was heard a thousand times.

Since no one wanted to say good-bye to loved ones and our motherland, "We'll see each other again" seemed more appropriate.

All the while, a jolly-sounding band played on, loud and a bit chaotic.

It was now 11:00 a.m. The loudspeaker blasted, "*La nave é in partenza!*" The boat was leaving. As the sleek, elegant liner slipped her moorings, the whistle blew steam against the red, white, and green bands on her funnel. Its blasts echoed against the hills of *Andrea Doria's* home port of Genoa.

I looked out at all the people wearing black, trying to spot Nonna Apollonia. Not wanting to make Nonna cry again, I didn't ask if she could see her.

And soon we had set sail.

The moment was finally here! I rejoiced that in ten days, I would be meeting my mother, who had reached the New World eight years earlier.

First Day at Sea

— *Tuesday, July 17* —

Piera

I looked up at the Mediterranean sky. The seagulls that had been escorting our country's cherished ocean liner were turning back to shore, knowing nature's boundaries by instinct. I looked back as far as I could along the side of the *Andrea Doria*. Her movement reminded me of a majestic swan. I knew we would be traveling in style.

The ship is moving fast. Will Nonna panic now? I was really worried.

"Let's go inside!" I demanded, hoping to get them away from looking down into the ocean. My Nonnis didn't share my thirst for exploring the interiors of the ship, but I pulled on their arms until they had to come with me.

On the way, we asked a lot of directions, and we finally found our cabins, numbers 412 and 416, right near each other. I immediately loved the cabin that Nonna and I were going to share. It had bunk beds, a sink, a bathroom—and a porthole!

"This is going to be so much fun! We get to watch the water and the fish."

Why is Nonna looking so scared? Nothing bad is going to happen.

Nonna howled and scolded me. "Get away from that window! It's dangerous!" Then she mumbled with a familiar sobbing sound as she put both hands to her head. *"Tanta acqua!"* I didn't share her fear of so much water, as she put it.

I ran out to see Nonno's cabin. He smiled at me but couldn't hide that he felt strange being on a moving liner. We had never even been on a small boat!

"Ho fame, Nonno." It was lunchtime, and I told him I was really hungry. Would they serve my favorite foods? I loved polenta with rabbit in wine sauce, a treat sometimes on Sundays. Or would it be something simple like fried potatoes and green beans?

We found our way to the dining room. I could barely keep my eyes in my face when I spotted the ice sculptures of glistening fish and mermaids on the buffet table. Then there were foods in all colors with aromas from a different world.

Is this really for us? I wondered. I was reassured that it was when a young man dressed in white from head to toe escorted us to our table. There were eight seats, and a family of four was already there. *We are going to sit with strangers?* I felt intimidated, and a terrible shyness took hold of me. I grabbed my Nonna's hand and pushed my body against hers, as if I wanted to take refuge beneath her wings. We had never eaten with strangers in our lives—never!

A sweet-looking lady, with a round belly on a small frame, stood up. The fact that she was pregnant made her special to Nonna; she had always adored women in this condition and was very fond of small children. The women in Pranzalito could sit together for hours in front of the fireplace, nursing their children, in a ritual of community, motherhood, and humanity all wrapped up in baby blankets.

"I'm Marge Henderson," the lady said, and she introduced her children. Pete, Randy, and Ilene smiled without much interest. I didn't smile at all.

Then something curious happened. Our table was asked to go get our own food. I assumed that this was what they did at restaurants. We had only eaten at home or at village feasts where they set food on our tables.

"Piera, take anything you want and put it on this plate," Nonna explained. "You've got to gain some weight so your mother doesn't think we've neglected you." She was always wanting me to eat, even when I wasn't hungry—which was my usual state. People in Pranzalito would snicker as my doting Nonna followed me around holding food in her hands in case, at any moment, I might decide to eat.

My grandma blamed all of my problems, especially being underweight, on missing my parents. Being really skinny, shy, and cranky was all because I didn't have parents. The fact is, I didn't miss my parents, because I didn't know them! I was perfectly happy just being with my Nonnis, but I didn't always feel well. Grandpa did his part to fatten me up by squirting milk from the cow's udders directly into my mouth. He'd joke around and keep squirting it even when I closed my mouth.

Today was different. I planned to eat everything I saw on the serving tables. I took Russian salad, seafood pasta, Gorgonzola cheese, and tiramisu for dessert. As we were returning to our table, I realized that there was music coming from somewhere. *Is it a radio like the one in our old kitchen?* Italian tunes made my Nonnis happy, especially Nonna, who loved to sing and to dance. Nonno never did either one.

Mrs. Henderson smiled again when we returned. "How old is Piera?" she asked Nonno, probably trying to bring him out of his quiet state.

"Nine and a half," he told her.

"Pete is twelve, Randy is ten, and Ilene is six," she offered. "And this one is going to be born in three months," she said as she rubbed her belly. "Have you been on a ship before?"

Nonno shook his head, and Nonna let out her usual howl of discomfort as her arm flew above her head.

"We're immigrating to America," she explained to Mrs. Henderson. "Piera's mother, baby sister, and new father are waiting for us. We're going to live together, at least for a while, until my husband and I find jobs. We were farmers. We don't know how to do anything else, but we didn't want Piera to travel alone, and we didn't want to be separated from her. We're the only parents she's ever known! Her mother left for America looking for a better life. Italy was really poor after the war ended, and she didn't think her daughter would have enough opportunities for education and work."

All of a sudden, after what seemed like Nonna's story hour, there was complete silence. I looked up from my delicious food and saw four faces staring at Nonna, as if they were trying to chew their food and swallow a difficult concept at the same time. Perhaps it was impossible to comprehend our unusual family situation.

Then we learned that the Hendersons were from Ohio. Mr. Henderson had won some kind of prize—a Fulbright scholarship in engineering, his wife told us. The family had lived in Torino, Italy, for a whole year together. And now they were excited to be returning to America.

Our getting-acquainted time at table 52 was abruptly interrupted by a young boy running past us and bumping into

Nonno's chair.

"Come back here, Patrick!" begged a mother at the next table. "Darlene and I will help you find the pool."

The boy was already out the door, having bumped into several occupied chairs on his way. His mother and older sister followed the human hurricane, looking apprehensive and embarrassed.

Mrs. Henderson grinned at the boy's folly and asked her children if they wanted to go swimming. "Why don't you bring Piera there? The children can all splash around together."

"Oh no!" Nonna exclaimed with a tone of anxiety and confusion. "Piera doesn't swim. We don't like water." It was an odd thing to say, since we were depending on it right now in order to reach our destination.

"Then come watch," Mrs. Henderson suggested.

We followed her and her children up the metal stairs. I wasn't ready to talk to them yet, but I thought to myself, *This is going to be a lot of fun. I hope Nonna brought my bathing suit!*

The mother and sister of that wild boy, Patrick, were already sitting on lounge chairs beside the pool, and Patrick was on the diving board ready to jump. The sun was hot, really hot, and I wanted to go into the turquoise water. The only water I had ever been in was Chiusella, the river that crossed our farmland. It was always chilly, and the rocks were slippery, but Nonna could watch me as she scrubbed sheets on a big rock. There were no rocks here, and the water felt perfect to the touch when I dipped in my finger. But I held tight onto Nonna's hand and cowered behind her.

From somewhere I heard, "Don't be chicken! Get your suit on!" It was Patrick beckoning me, if not daring me. *He's nine, too. Why can't I be as brave as he is?* Now I felt really shy, especially since we were always needing someone to translate for us between English and Italian. Nonna led us to some chairs near Patrick's family.

Patrick's slender, energetic-looking mother extended her hand as she shaded her face. "I'm Germina Marino, and this is my daughter, Darlene," she said. The teenage girl gave a smile that matched the warmth of her chestnut hair. Mrs. Marino seemed friendly and outgoing and immediately put us at ease. "And that's my impatient son, Patrick." She looked at me recoiling in the huge chair, then added, "Don't let him rush you, *bella*. He's got to be doing something all the time. Just can't stay still."

I was momentarily relieved—until I heard an unidentifiable animal noise, accompanied by a big splash that got us all. It was that wild boy. We wiped the water off ourselves and listened to Mrs. Marino tell one of the funniest stories we'd ever heard.

"Since I'm a 'war bride'—I married an American soldier—my family in Italy invited me and the children for a visit. Four weeks ago, when the *Doria* was about to leave dock, my son was nowhere to be found. My husband even came onto the boat to search for him. An officer announced his name on the ship loudspeaker. That devil was busy climbing up to the funnel; he opened the windows and kept banging on it so he could wave to people on shore. When he finally heard his name, he didn't know where to report. A crew member took him by the arm and made him face his father and the captain. If the captain hadn't been there, that boy would have gotten a good licking!"

We all laughed, knowing that she was embellishing the story, but we wanted to hear more. Nonna was holding her stomach and wiping tears from her eyes as Patrick's mother continued.

"But the ship had already left the dock, so my husband had to ride back to shore in a tugboat. All of this just added to the humiliation of getting a pizza slice dropped on his new suit while he was waving good-bye from shore earlier. I hope I can get that son of mine back to New York safe!"

I couldn't remember the last time Nonna and Nonno had smiled. It wasn't in Pranzalito, and it wasn't on the way to Genoa. *I really hope Mrs. Marino tells more funny stories tomorrow.*

There was an entire sun-drenched afternoon ahead of us. I asked my Nonnis if we could walk around. Nonna was nervous at this idea but realized that no matter where she was, she would be surrounded by water. Was her fear based on when her daughter, an only child, had almost drowned in the town well when she was three? But men had crawled down, holding on to a rope, to rescue the screaming girl. Or was it because she had to take cows to pasture in a field just beyond the river? She always warned me to stay right next to her as we jumped from rock to rock together. I didn't dare ask the reason; it would just cause her to relive her fear-filled past.

Now we were strolling—all three of us together—and I liked it. Throngs of people had already discovered the "lido lounge"; the bar was decorated with mythological figures that I knew nothing about. People held colorful drinks in their hands, pinks, reds, blues; some had swizzle sticks and umbrellas in them. I wanted one but opted for more exploring time.

Then we saw a funny sight, unlike anything I was used to: three nuns giggling on the deck as they struggled with their billowing habits that were getting in the way of a long stick. They were trying to move a round black object over some numbers—I learned later that the game was called shuffleboard. One nun instructed the one pushing the stick, "Sister Angelica, just crumple the habit with your left hand, pull on it, then push quickly on the puck." They continued to giggle as the wind tossed their long black veils in swirls, sometimes covering their faces.

They made me think of the nuns who had taught me catechism after school in Pranzalito. They'd brought books with picture stories to teach us about devils, guardian angels, and, of course, God. Their faces were always stern. I didn't think nuns were allowed to giggle. Besides, I thought it would hurt to move their faces inside their tight headdresses.

Around the corner was a room just for children. Its walls were painted with bright-colored animals doing funny things. There was a kangaroo sniffing a pineapple, a monkey photographing a flower, bugs dancing to clowns holding whips. Small children played and laughed as their parents watched.

A father introduced himself to my Nonnis. "I'm Rick Holmes. This is my wife, Helga, and my twins. We're headed back to the States after a year in Saudi Arabia." He pointed to the buggy beside him. I peeked in and saw two very small babies. "Two months old. The other three are all over the place," Mr. Holmes added as he looked around the room. Then he called for the other three to come meet us. *From Saudi Arabia? They look like the rest of us,* I thought as I remembered drawings of children with veils and long dresses in a geography book. Nonno would explain later that they were Americans, but Mr. Holmes had worked for an oil company in Saudi Arabia.

"We're going to see the Walt Disney movie *Living Desert* now," Mr. Holmes said. "With this big family, it's good to have something that makes the afternoon pass quickly. Would you like to join us?" We barely understood what a Walt Disney movie was, so my Nonnis shook their heads and said good-bye.

We headed for the game room instead. Four young men were holding paddles and hitting a small white ball back and forth across a green wooden table. *I want to do that, too,* I thought. *I hope they'll ask us to play.* They laughed when the ball went above their heads and hit a lady's face as she sat in a stuffed chair. The lady just smiled and threw the ball back. They said something I didn't recognize; it must have meant thank you. Nonna looked at Nonno and said, "Tedeschi." That meant that they came from Germany.

Nearby, two priests seemed to be engaged in a lively banter. They held cards in their hands. We learned that they were Fathers Gardner and Kennedy, from Illinois and Michigan. They were playing a game called bridge. They nodded a friendly hello to us.

Not knowing how to play any of the games, my Nonnis and I decided to go back out onto the sunny deck.

I put on my wide-rimmed, black-and-white polka-dot sunglasses, which my mother had sent me. This was a good thing because I could watch without seeming to stare at an awkward encounter between a waiter and a passenger. The passenger was reading a book while stretched out on a lounge chair.

The waiter, all dressed in white, approached him and asked politely, "May I bring you a beverage, Mr. Murphy?"

The man, who appeared older than my Nonno, looked up as if he was distressed by the simple question. He shook his head and turned to the next page of his book.

The waiter asked again, perhaps thinking that the man was hard of hearing. "What can I get you from the lounge, sir?"

The man seemed troubled as he tried to readjust his body in the chair.

The waiter looked puzzled and confused. He bowed and turned to the next passenger but kept looking back at Mr. Murphy.

My Nonnis looked at each other. I was almost happy that Nonna had found someone else who wasn't happy on the ship.

Why is Mr. Murphy acting this way? Is he scared of something? Maybe he's deaf or ill?

Conversations and the Captain

First Class

On the higher decks of the ship, First Class passengers had finished their sumptuous meal, with pasta dishes and a full buffet that included wild boar, roast lamb with mint sauce, glazed duckling, and ox tongue.

Many passengers felt invited to indulge in the relaxed, plush atmosphere of the Lido Deck as they adjusted their walking and their digestion to the undulating roll of the ship. Families, single people, and clergy took communal delight in soaking up the warm sun or taking refuge in the lounge. An adult favorite was Campari, while a pink fruity drink teased the children's taste buds as they wondered what secret ingredients made up such a delight.

Others chose to stroll along the teak corridors of the glass-lined Promenade Deck two levels below. From there, they could walk almost the entire circumference of the ship. Or they might relax on the wooden lounge chairs positioned for a full view of the ocean.

At the very top of the vessel was the Belvedere Deck, named for its beautiful view. Passengers were surrounded by endless open sky and water.

The Yates and Campi families had met at lunch and were chatting while sitting in a circle of comfortable Art Deco armchairs. Richard and Victoria Yates were traveling with their son, Daniel, age sixteen, and their daughter, Margaret, who was fourteen. Mr. Yates, a tall, scholarly-looking gentleman, was a highly respected naval architect and marine engineer. The family was bringing Margaret back to the States for prep school. Among all of the ships they traveled on regularly for Mr. Yates's work, they chose the *Andrea Doria* for its beauty, comfort, and safety.

Carmelo Campi was the Madrid correspondent for the *New York Times*. He and his wife, Josephine, were accompanying their daughter Lisa, whom he had adopted from Josephine's previous marriage, to a boarding school in Boston. Their eight-year-old, Julie, was also traveling with them.

Mr. Campi realized that he had struck journalistic gold to be traveling with a maritime scientist and an expert on the *Andrea*

Doria. "I'm planning to write a feature article about traveling on the *Doria*," the Mediterranean-looking middle-aged journalist explained, hoping to extract some real information from Richard Yates. After all, Yates was the chairman of European operations for the American Bureau of Shipping. "I assume that the ABS has certified the *Andrea Doria*," Mr. Campi asked in his charming way, assuming that the answer would be yes.

Before Mr. Yates could reply, his son, Daniel, interjected, "It passed all of its requirements in safety standards and construction."

Daniel, a tall teen with a shiny crewcut, caught a glimpse of his mother beaming with pride. He blushed a little. Victoria, a slender, refined-looking woman, added a footnote to the chitchat: "My son is doing an internship under his dad's supervision. He's getting quite keen on ship design." Mr. Yates nodded, smiling in agreement.

Mr. Campi knew that he would have plenty of fodder for his feature article. But he would have to wait for the next social gathering. Mr. Yates placed a hand on his son's shoulder and said, "We have an appointment on the bridge with the captain himself. I want Daniel to meet him and his crew so they'll understand why we're investigating everything from the Promenade Deck down to the bowels of their ship for the next nine days."

"Let me know if you find any rivets missing," Mr. Campi joked. The journalist was referring to the rivet failures on the famous sunken *Titanic*. "The *Times* wants real tooth-and-nail details for this article."

As the father and son left, Margaret Yates and Lisa Campi seemed to be forming a friendship. They were the same age, fourteen, and felt comfortable together through their parents' new relationship onboard.

Captain Piero Calamai, six feet tall, stood at the foremost space of the vessel. He looked out at the sea, thinking about his relationship with the *Andrea Doria*. He had courted the three-year-old Grande Dame of the Sea, whose architectural lines made her look as sleek as a yacht, since his wife had brought home an advertising flyer, which he had read with delight.

"Into this lovely ship has gone all the proud craftsmanship born of centuries of tradition . . . every modern device for your pleasure and convenience. From the glistening mosaics of her three magnificent outdoor swimming pools to radar; from gleaming Venetian crystal to air-conditioning; from breathtaking tapestries to modern turbines that drive her sleek hull at 23 express-speed knots. . . . She is the glory of yesterday . . . the newest of today. She is the *Andrea Doria*."

The captain was a proud man. At only fifty-two, he'd been promoted to the flagship of the Italian Line and the symbol of its rebirth: half of its fleet had been destroyed by bombings during World War II. Master Calamai was intimately familiar with the war; he had served as captain of the new Italian battleship *Italia*. Toward the end of the conflict, in 1943, he had surrendered the ship to the Allies. But the master mariner was most proud for having saved the battleship *Caio Duilio;* he had run it aground on a sandbar after the British torpedoed it in 1940.

This trip was to be the last for the *Andrea Doria* under his command. Upon the ship's return to Genoa, he was to become master of the *Doria's* sister ship, the *Cristoforo Colombo*. For Calamai, senior master of the Italian Line, it was the high point of forty years at sea. He had already commanded the highly prized liners *Saturnia, Ugolino, Paolo Toscanelli,* and *Santa Cruz*.

With engine telegraphs ordering *tutta forza*, or full speed, and the wheelhouse doors opened to the breezes of the warm afternoon, the *Andrea Doria* was making its 101st trip across the Atlantic. It steamed ahead at its maximum speed: 23 knots.

The captain left the bridge of command, walked inside his office, and sat at his beautifully varnished desk. He noted important data in his personal logbook: 1,134 passengers (190 First Class, 267 Cabin Class, 677 Third Class), 572 crew, 401 tons of freight, 522 pieces of shipped gear, 1,754 bags of mail, nine automobiles.

He also wrote down, "Lifeboat Drill: 10:00 a.m."

Only the captain and a few select passengers were privy to one of its secret passengers: the Chrysler "Norseman." It was a "concept car," one of the first aerodynamic cars built out of aluminum to reduce weight. Hand-built by Ghia in Italy for Chrysler, it was quietly destined for the 1957 auto-show circuit in the United States. Said to be worth $200,000, the special vehicle had been loaded in a crate—both for protection and for concealment. It was parked among other automotive royalty in the garage, including Rolls-Royces and a Mercury Turnpike Cruiser.

Calamai debated in his mind whether he would share this information with Richard and Daniel Yates. After all, he was allowing them to examine every detail of his ship for the young man's benefit. But would his automobile clients object to having them visit the garage? He would soon make this delicate decision.

Lifeboat Drill

— Wednesday, July 18 —

Piera

"Wake up, Piera!" I found myself looking up at Nonna, with her loving brown eyes and wavy brown hair that looked like mine. "There's going to be a lifeboat drill today, so we need to go to breakfast very soon."

Breakfast? I don't remember having dinner last night! The smooth forward movement on calm ocean waves had lulled me into a sound slumber. As I put on my favorite green skirt (green was my favorite color), white blouse, and red and white shoes, Nonna clipped a delicate white bow to my banana curls. They were the same ones she had styled in Pranzalito by heating a curling iron on our black wood stove.

During this familiar ritual, I realized how different my life was now. I would never return to simple summer delights of getting up, eating breakfast, going to find my friends to play hide-and-seek in the tall grass, climb plum trees, pick buttercups and violets along the brook, or go to the river to catch frogs.

I missed my friends and wished we could do the lifeboat drill together. Nonno sounded serious when he had explained the procedure yesterday. "In case we're sinking, we get into the small boats. They row us away from the ship so we're safe."

It would be fun to get into the little boats, I thought at first. But I hoped it would never happen at night; that would be too scary. *And what if there were sharks?* I shuddered but shrugged my fears away, thinking that the captain would never let us ride where there were sharks.

At breakfast, as Nonno sipped at his tiny espresso cup, my heart thumped hard at the sound of a shrieking whistle. It hollered six short blasts and then a single long moan. Nonna looked alarmed and put her hands to her head.

"It's fine, Mrs. Burzio," said Mrs. Henderson in an effort to calm my anxious grandmother. "Let's just go up to the Boat Deck for the lifeboat drill." I was relieved at Mrs. Henderson's maternal ways. Although I was scared of this—one more new experience—I walked hand-in-hand with my Nonnis without tears or pouting. We first went to our cabins, grabbed our life vests, tugged on the straps, and rushed back to the corridor.

I watched other families climb the stairs with a calm sense

of urgency; I realized that this was important. When we finally stopped clanking up what seemed like hundreds of steps, we stopped at a long corridor lined with a very long row of windows. But where were the lifeboats? Someone pointed up. There they were, eight of them, hanging over the sea. They frightened me. *I don't want to get in those! How can we get into them, anyway? It's too hard to do!* I got teary-eyed.

After we'd been standing in the glass-lined corridor for a long time, a young man broke the quietness and asked, "Where is the crew? Isn't anyone going to show us what to do?" Just as I looked up to study the situation, I saw a small person struggling to free himself from a crew member's grasp.

The only officer in sight approached Mrs. Marino with one arm raised to punctuate every point he was making. "*Signora,* you have to keep an eye on your son. He's getting into forbidden parts of the ship. He could get hurt—badly hurt. I just pulled him out of a lifeboat. He could have slipped and dropped into the ocean. He's a menace!"

Patrick pulled his head free and shifted from one foot to the other. "I need to know how to get my bike into one of these in case the ship sinks!" he protested.

He didn't seem to care that everyone was smirking at his foolishness. Someone quipped, "Who would be so stupid to get into a lifeboat with a bike? Now, if it were a car—" The last statement seemed to ease the crowd's apprehension, except for

Mrs. Marino's.

"If you don't stop all your nonsense right now—" She paused. Was she wondering how to punish Patrick, or was she suddenly embarrassed to be identified as that rascal's mother?

Her daughter, Darlene, had obviously been assessing the situation and spoke up. "Patrick, you don't even know where your bike *is!*" she said mockingly.

"I'll find it, dopey."

By now, Patrick's mother must have felt thoroughly ashamed. She looked angry. She grabbed Patrick by the arm as if she wanted to move him out of sight. I heard her complaining to Darlene, "Good Lord, I hope I can get this boy back to New York in one piece. If your father finds out about today's episode, he'll never let us take Patrick to Italy again."

To my amazement, Nonna giggled. Patrick's escapade seemed to have diverted her attention from the serious lifeboat drill.

Will Patrick get a spanking? Will the captain find out about this? None of my friends ever acted like this. He's not afraid of anything!

⚜

During lunch, the dining room was buzzing with talk about the lifeboat drill. Everyone seemed too preoccupied to admire, as they had done yesterday, the beautiful drawings of the old port of Genoa that adorned the walls.

Two priests and three nuns were sitting at the table next to us. Young Father Kennedy, who was returning to Michigan after a year in Rome, said, "Praise the Lord for lifeboats that can hold all of us should there be a disaster!"

Father Gardner, the middle-aged priest, was obviously less enthusiastic about what he had seen. "Unfortunately, I don't think we would know how to board them. I even had trouble putting on my life vest."

One of the nuns who had been playing shuffleboard said, "The life vest wouldn't go over my wide starched collar." She chuckled, seeming like the kind of person who saw humor in every situation. "If there is ever a need to wear it, I'll have to remember to remove the collar first."

The younger priest agreed with a smile and added, "Did you see how flustered Mr. Murphy was when he tried to put on his life vest? He was perspiring so much that he couldn't find the buckles through the sweat pouring off his forehead!"

The other priest offered earnestly, "I prayed for him. For some reason, he couldn't even face the lifeboats. He just looked toward the wall, like an ice statue."

At the priest's comment, all five of them made the sign of the cross. I wasn't sure if it had to do with Mr. Murphy's anxiety or if it was just part of saying grace.

Then Sister Angelica asked, "What if we ask Mr. Murphy to join us for meals when we see him?"

Daniel and the Super Ship

— Wednesday, July 18 —

First Class

The Mediterranean Sea glistened as the sun kissed it with blazing rays. Small ripples, dancing to the music of the breezes, covered the deep blue water and twinkled back at the sun. White wispy clouds, almost absent from this perfect summer scene, were hints of contrast against the vastness of blue.

The captain gazed from his office windows, which arched around him. He was wondering about the lifeboat drill. Had all of the passengers reported to their muster stations? Had the crew been attentive to them?

Later that afternoon, he would focus on connecting with his staff, he thought. It was a long chain that included mechanical, hotel, entertainment, and other services for the comfort and safety of the passengers. He decided that he would make his rounds after receiving two special guests in his office.

A warm greeting interrupted his thoughts.

"Good afternoon, Captain!" An eager young man stuck out his hand.

"*Buon giorno,*" the captain replied, almost quietly, realizing that he had been thinking in Italian. He switched to English and extended his hand to Mr. Yates, adding, "I was looking forward to your visit. My office alerted me of your father-son project."

Mr. Yates explained, "Daniel is doing his school internship with me. He wants to follow in my footsteps and pursue a degree in naval architecture and marine engineering."

The young man was dressed in his usual white crew-neck vest, a light blue shirt, and light blue khakis—similar to the uniform at his school in London. Since his father was chairman of European operations of the American Bureau of Shipping, Daniel also wore a gold pin with the initials "ABS."

"I plan to build a structure for a ship that can sail the seas without damage from collisions, storms, and even bombs—like a super ship," Daniel said.

The captain was delighted by the young maritime-scientist-to-be, but he cautioned, "Bombs can do a lot of destruction. I'm not sure how ships could overcome such damage and stay afloat."

Daniel recalled what he'd heard about the captain's experience and survival on a battleship. He felt a little embarrassed to have brought up the subject.

"Would you like a tour of the bridge?" the captain asked.

"Yes! I'd like to see everything. Dad explained some things, but I need to see them in action."

Mr. Yates was proud of his son's enthusiasm. He was happy that the boy had already found his calling. They followed Captain Calamai from one navigation instrument to another. Daniel appeared to take careful mental note of every instrument he saw along the way, even stroking some of them gently: gauges, levers, bells, circuit boards, wheels, and screens of every size, mostly gray and black.

The captain made some introductions. "I'd like you to meet my bridge staff, starting with First Officer Franchini. Then there is Second Officer Giannini. They rotate during good weather; I like to have both of them with me during storms and fog conditions. One can never be too cautious." Daniel was impressed with the captain's prudent ways. "This is my helmsman. He's not allowed to take his eyes off the wheel." Calamai said it lightheartedly, but he demanded proper ship navigation. "And in the radio room, we have the officer who communicates my messages. He communicates them to the engine room and other parts of the ship. He can also send Morse-code messages throughout the Atlantic."

Daniel, wanting to steer the tour himself a bit, asked, "And what is your main job, Captain?"

"To provide safe passage for my passengers and crew." The captain was known for his stoicism and preferred to use words sparingly for emphasis.

"My dad tells me that the *Doria* is equipped with state-of-the-art technology," Daniel said as he inspected one of the two radar scopes.

"We have two radars for maximum safety. They locate vessels of every size in any weather. Then we have a gyrocompass for direction . . . and an inclinometer." Daniel noted that it read 0.5, and he understood that the ship's movement created a slight incline.

Mr. Yates added, "The *Doria* wouldn't sink unless the inclinometer were to read fifteen degrees—and that's unlikely ever to happen."

The three walked inside a glass partition to a table displaying a large chart. The captain made a notation with a wax pencil, plotting the ship's course.

Daniel was distracted by flashing lights on a board. "What do these do?" he asked.

"They indicate the position of watertight doors. The lights tell me which are open or closed. There are twelve watertight compartments on the ship."

Daniel remembered his father showing him a diagram of the way a ship was compartmentalized to resist flooding in case another object penetrated it. It also increased the ship's overall strength. He had read that this method dated back to the second century and had been used in the warships of Kublai Khan.

Mr. Yates, who knew the *Doria's* structure with even more expertise than the captain, added, "Up to two adjacent compartments could be flooded before the *Doria* would sink."

That's it! Daniel thought. *This is the secret to my unsinkable ship.* He noted silently that he would build a ship that could withstand more compartments flooding.

"Here is the pass to tour my ship. Show this to any crew member, and it will give you full access." The captain added, "You are free to visit all eleven decks—but the car garage is off limits, even to most of my staff."

Daniel wanted to ask why, but he thought he knew. The Chrysler "Norseman" concept car had been the buzz in the news for weeks in London and in Italy.

Fun—and Prayers—for Travelers

— *Thursday, July 19* —

Piera

Last night, Nonna had nightmares again. She tossed, turned, and threw covers on and off all night long, moaning about the ocean that was transporting her to America. I said a prayer she had taught me for when I was worried: "Dear Lord, share your peace with those who are seeking . . ." I wanted Nonna to relax and have some fun like the other passengers.

It crossed my mind that she might be suffering from indigestion, something she often complained about. In fact, in Pranzalito, she would warm a black iron on the wood stove and wrap it in a towel; then she would "iron" her stomach and chest until loud belches escaped from inside her.

On the ship, it was hard to decide what to eat at dinner, and how much, since there were so many choices on the menu. It was an adventure discovering new flavors. I became fond of mayonnaise and cranberry and other delicious fruits: pineapple, dates, cantaloupe. Nonno discovered new wines; some were white and pink and very different from the red wine he used to make from our grapes. Nonna did indulge in sweets (along with me!) and became very fond of tiramisu, a light, creamy, coffee-flavored cake, and some heavy, sour dairy drink called buttermilk.

This was going to be a brand-new day full of adventures. We had heard of the possibilities, but up to now, my Nonnis' limitations, whether from shyness or fear, had kept them on a rather boring routine.

I was excited when Nonno came to our cabin and announced, "I've been invited to play cards! I'll be going to a room at the back of the ship; it's called the lounge."

I hope it's safe back there. Will Nonno bring his briefcase?

"Nonno, can I come, too, *per piacere,*" I begged with a loud "please." "I could watch your briefcase while you play!" I knew my grandfather's pride and appealed to it. At every meal and on every stroll, Nonno was the protector of all of our immigration documents and money, which he thought needed guarding at all times. He had told me, "No one can enter America without a passport and money."

He looked at Nonna, who didn't seem to object to the card game, and replied, "Only if you stay right next to me." Since

I couldn't imagine exploring this floating city alone, I said, "*Si. Grazie!*" I was happy to spend some time alone with my Nonno, whom I loved dearly. He was the only "father" I had ever known. One time, years earlier, I had tried to address him as *Papà;* he became angry and explained firmly that he was not my father and that I should not call him that again. It was confusing—and hurtful—since my friends all called the heads of their households *Papà.* Why was it different for me?

After another delicious breakfast of something called "bacon" and "Philadelphia cream cheese" spread on bread, we left Nonna with Mrs. Marino's family, with whom she had become friendly. Nonno looked a little nervous as we headed to the stern, but he seemed intent on impressing other men with his new suit, tie, and hat.

Several men greeted us with brief handshakes and their names, looking as if they had better things to do than exchange pleasantries. They looked much younger than my grandfather. We sat down and watched the cards being shuffled. Within minutes, the game became a setting for manly conversations. Around the table in this modern-looking lounge, old tales with new plots began to surface.

Alberto had a burly body but looked somewhat frail and spoke softly. "I was a machinist in Sicily but couldn't do my job because I have a heart problem. My wife is pregnant. So my brother in Connecticut said there is a special surgery in

America. After, he has a job lined up for me."

I was happy for him. *I'm glad I'm going to America, too,* I thought. *If Nonno gets sick, doctors can perform miracles on him.*

It was Ezio's turn to deal, so he spoke next. "I sold my farm in Piacenza, where my seven brothers and sisters live. I hated leaving them, but my wife is already in New York, and she found a job for me as a dishwasher. Maybe later I'll be a chef." He lifted his suit lapel and lightheartedly added, "My family hired a tailor to make me seven new suits. They've seen Americans in Piacenza and think their clothes are ugly." There were nods and grins of agreement from all. "But where am I going to wear all the suits?"

The players smiled. They probably hadn't thought about what they would be doing in their brand-new clothes. What was important, Nonno had said often about dressing, is for immigrants to make a *bella figura,* a good impression.

It was now Giovanni's turn to share the hand that had been dealt to him. It was a sad story, and I listened with only an inkling of understanding. "I'm traveling with my wife and three girls: four, three, and two. My wife is homesick and seasick; she cries a lot. But we want to get to New York and make a better life for our daughters." Giovanni was obviously a good family man, like the other card players. We watched him wipe a tear from each eye as he recalled tragic memories. "I owned a tailor shop in Toritto, near Bari. It was prosperous because our port was the home for Allied ships on the Adriatic during the war."

Giovanni pulled out his handkerchief, wiped his face in circles, and continued. "Enemy planes bombed everything. Oh, *Dio*. They exploded a Liberty ship with mustard gas . . . that beautiful city from medieval times reduced to rubble. They called it the second Pearl Harbor."

We all listened with empathy as Giovanni had more anguish to share. "It became hard to make ends meet, hard to find food sometimes. When an immigrant returned to visit me from America, he said, 'I make good money in America, and I'm just a clerk! My friends think I'm a big shot.' So I'm transplanting my whole family. Maybe I'll even have enough money to sponsor other immigrants."

I hoped that Giovanni really would become a "big shot," but my patience for listening had reached its limits. I turned away from the card table and another game, to look at a picture on the wall. Two knights in armor and on horseback were dueling on top of a floor that looked just like a chess game. *I wonder which one will win,* I asked myself, studying the way they were holding their jousting poles and noticing that they each had a damsel waiting, holding a long headdress.

A sympathetic waiter, seeing me holding my head in my hands to save my energy for listening, brought me a beverage. It was green! He told me it was *anguria,* watermelon. I had never tasted such a flavor, but I loved it and slurped it too fast;

it didn't last through Nonno's immigrant story.

"My wife and I had a farm at the foot of the Alps, with cows, pigs, chickens, and rabbits. But Piera's mother kept asking for her daughter to join her in Detroit, Michigan. She's been there for eight years, and we've raised her daughter. Our priest offered Piera a plane ticket through a Catholic agency, but Piera said that airplanes are dangerous. We're lucky to get tickets on this ship. It's not going to carry immigrants much longer. Airplanes are taking over, you know."

As he spoke, the furrow in his forehead seemed to be growing deeper. "Besides, we don't want to be separated from the girl we love like a daughter. So, to make everybody happy, we sold everything, even the farmlands and the vineyards." Nonno looked very sad—not happy at all. I got a terrible feeling in my stomach, knowing it had nothing to do with the *anguria*. I didn't know what to say to make Nonno feel better, but I thought, *I hope he'll be happy in America.*

It would be clear to me later that this had been more than a card game; it had been like a therapy session, where the card players could weigh their decisions of sacrifice with those of other immigrants. It was their way of understanding the cards they had been dealt and gaining a perspective on how to play them in the New World.

By now, I had started missing my Nonna. I was ready for fun with other children and people who were ready for adven-

FUN—AND PRAYERS—FOR TRAVELERS

ture on the ship, before we all got to what some were calling the promised land.

Nonno lifted the briefcase from his lap, shook the paisanos' hands, and led me to the pool, where Nonna was waiting with the five Hendersons, Mrs. Marino, Darlene, and Patrick. *I hope he does something funny today.* Of course, Patrick was already in his swimsuit; it had bikes of every color printed on it. I noticed that he had a long face instead of his usual carefree look. He protested to his mother, "Jeepers, Ma, why can't I keep my bike in my cabin?"

Mrs. Marino shook her head, seemingly more interested in reading *Life* magazine. Darlene peered out of her own *Seventeen* magazine to add, "Ye gads, why would you want to do that?"

"Mind your own beeswax, dopey!" He turned to his mother again. "That boy I beat up in Yonkers jinxed me and my stuff. He said, 'I hope your ship sinks and you lose your pants!'" Then he made his last plea. "Ma, if the ship starts to sink, I wanna save my bike!"

Mrs. Marino, not even looking up, answered sweetly, "We'll talk about it later, dear."

At this point, Patrick noticed us. He asked me, "Did you bring your swimsuit?"

Nonna spoke up for me. "We don't like water."

Patrick made a funny face and replied, "Then you're in the wrong place, lady." His mother asked him to speak more

49

politely to adults, but he added, "We're on the ocean, Ma!"

He was right, I thought. And, besides, I had bathed in a river. I asked my grandmother if I had a bathing suit; she nodded reluctantly.

"I dare you to get into the water!" Patrick yelled just before taking a running leap and jumping in, holding his knees to his head. It looked scary but fun.

I wish I was that brave. I feel so much younger than him. How did he get to be so "old" at nine?

Nonna had run out of excuses based on Patrick's unquestionable logic. She finally said, "We'll put your suit on after lunch."

I looked at Darlene, who was clapping in small, rapid movements. She pointed out that the pool had Scottish designs in a mosaic pattern of green and white. Since I loved green more than any other color, I knew I would like the pool.

As we soaked up the Mediterranean sun and the ship rocked and rolled gently, we heard a courteous greeting.

"*Buon giorno,*" someone said with a funny-sounding accent. "Hello. I'm Richard Yates, and this is my son, Daniel. He is studying the design of the *Andrea Doria*. After college, he plans to be a naval architect and marine engineer—like his father," he added with a pleasant grin.

Darlene began translating for my Nonnis and me. But I still didn't understand what they were saying. It didn't matter. I focused on how dapper they looked. The father, a jolly fellow, sported navy-blue shoes and trousers, topped by a white sweater over a crisp white shirt. I tried to understand the circle embossed on the sweater, but all I recognized were the letters ABS. Daniel was dressed a lot like his father, but he was wearing some kind of gold pin on his vest; three letters on it also read ABS.

Mr. Yates told Mrs. Marino that Daniel was sixteen, to which she replied, "My Darlene here is fourteen."

Daniel was gazing at Darlene, seemingly fascinated, as she continued to translate, but he quickly became serious as he explained directly to her, "I'm going to build the first unsinkable ship."

This statement brought a look of sudden bewilderment to my Nonna. "But I was told the *Andrea Doria* is unsinkable!" she exclaimed.

Mr. Yates tried to calm my shocked grandmother. "Don't worry, *Signora*. She's built with all the latest technology, even radar to prevent collisions. The *Doria* is practically unsinkable."

Nonna didn't appear comforted. I looked out at the horizon. *How could there possibly be a collision with another ship on such a wide ocean?*

But the dialogue about "unsinkable" versus "practically unsinkable" was not yet over. Patrick had been listening the whole time, waiting to put in his zinger before he flew down the slide into the pool. "They said the *Titanic* was unsinkable, too, and look what happened! I saw the movie, and I *saw* the

Titanic sink. She ran into an iceberg that opened her up like a sardine can."

Darlene looked at her brother and said, "The *Titanic* movie was made for Hollywood; they exaggerate things." She looked up at the others and explained, "He's talking about the new film *A Night to Remember*." Mr. Yates and Daniel nodded in agreement.

Daniel kept smiling at Darlene as if he were studying her. *Maybe he hasn't seen the movie, either, and wants to hear more,* I thought.

Mr. Yates looked proud as he placed his hand on his son's shoulder and said, "We're headed for the engine room to study what makes this ship move."

Patrick was again on top of the slide, actually smiling, something rare to see on his face. He always acted bored and rebellious. Now he slid downward, pounding on his chest like a caveman mustering his courage to face a dangerous expedition. To my surprise, no one seemed to notice him.

We all waved good-bye to Daniel and Mr. Yates.

Mrs. Marino added, "Good luck with your studies, young man. Come back and visit us and tell us what you learned."

Daniel nodded heartily. He shook Darlene's hand, waving at the rest of us. Patrick left the pool. I was surprised, since he had dared me to swim.

We didn't have time to reflect on the encounter or wonder why Patrick had left the pool. Looking up toward the sun, I saw the outline of a woman holding a child by the hand. I thought she looked different from the other women but couldn't pinpoint why. Then I realized her bathing suit had two pieces! *Wow! I wonder what Nonna thinks. I like it.*

"*Buon giorno,*" she said warmly, extending her hand to each grown-up around the pool. "I'm Laura Dunes, and this is my daughter, Mariana." The little girl clung to her mother while my Nonna did her usual routine with children. She giggled, pinched the girl's cheeks, talked to her in a high voice, and complimented her. "*Che bella bambina!*" Fortunately for me, my grandmother thought that all children were beautiful and special.

"I've seen you in the dining room," the young, blond, blue-eyed woman said. "I sit at a nearby table."

Mrs. Henderson, in her warm way, welcomed her to our circle of pool friends. "Do join us, please." She introduced Mariana to her three children, who asked the little girl to join them.

Then something amazing happened. Mrs. Dunes, who had a very lovely figure, stretched out her arms, jumped off the side of the pool, and plunged in. She proceeded to swim back and forth across the pool without stopping. *She's really great,* I thought. *She reminds me of a dolphin the way she leaps in and out of the water, then swims through it. I want to learn to do that, too.*

The afternoon was passing by quickly. I looked at my Nonnis; their uneasy expressions told me they still weren't convinced that they should be on the ship.

⚜

The ship's chapel was pretty, but I felt that it didn't hold a candle to my church in Pranzalito. I always loved the salmon-colored walls, the ornate marble altar with gold candelabras, and the sculpture of Jesus on the cross to remind everyone of why we were there. The side walls had coves holding statues of various saints and, of course, the Virgin Mary. The floor was of marbleized tiles, giving our feet a chill in the winter. But the air was warmed with the familiar smell of incense. I was sure that Nonno and Nonna were missing our village "jewel" by now.

Perhaps for this reason but probably more because of how Patrick had alarmed my grandparents, Nonna said that we needed to go to the chapel and pray. It wasn't easy for us to find our way to the Foyer Deck, but fortunately, many passengers spoke Italian when they offered directions.

Nonna pulled out her crystal rosary and held the beads with a nervous rubbing motion while her lips moved ever so lightly. It was a familiar ritual, but this time it appeared more intense, if not somehow desperate. Nonno simply clasped his hands and knelt on the walnut pew.

I felt fidgety. I wanted to be there for a reason, but I didn't have one. I usually liked praying, but this chapel in the center of the ship seemed impersonal. To pass time, I studied the three painted panels that adorned the altar. I turned next to the side walls; they were lined with panels depicting scenes from old Genoa.

Then I noticed something really interesting. On the other side of the aisle, Sister Angelica was kneeling and praying with an older man, Mr. Murphy, the same one we had seen perspiring so much during the lifeboat drill. Kneeling on the other side of him were the other two nuns. Were they protecting him?

Mr. Murphy, who had a shiny round bald spot on his head, looked nervous, really nervous. He held a Bible before him and read, skipping around from section to section. Then he sat back, closed the Bible, seemed to say a prayer, and rubbed his hands hard, as if washing them. I watched as he kept alternating between mouthing a prayer and rubbing his hands. Every so often, he also pressed his fingers on a white envelope tucked into his shirt pocket.

Sister Angelica glanced at him from around her long veil, which covered a tightly bound white wrap. Her skin wrinkled each time she turned toward the older man. Many questions crossed my mind as I twitched and stirred. *Who is that man? Why does Sister Angelica pray with him?*

Down in the Engine Room

— *Thursday, July 19* —

First Class

Daniel had looked forward to this day ever since his father had proposed that he do an internship on the *Andrea Doria*. He remembered him saying, "The bridge and the engine room are the two most important aspects of ship navigation. They're very different from each other. The bridge is clean, airy, and quiet, but the engine room is smelly, enclosed, and noisy."

After meeting some Third Class passengers, Daniel and Mr. Yates found the crew access door, which led downward passing several grated stairwells.

"We're headed below the ocean surface, son," Mr. Yates said. "Things are going to get noisy when we reach the bottom."

Daniel felt uneasy. Sounds were changing as they descended;

even their steps sounded more constrained, more muffled. But it wasn't until they opened the large, heavy metal door with its special knob that Daniel finally understood what his dad meant by "noisy."

With anxious eyes, he looked at his father and shouted above the chugging of pumps, the whirling of turbines, and the banging of propellers. In some areas, it sounded like being in a steel drum with a sledgehammer hitting its surface. "Are you sure it's safe for us down here?"

"Yes, son. Many men run the ship from down here. You'll see."

Daniel's heart was racing with trepidation at being in such an out-of-the-ordinary place. *Such foreign and enormous machinery . . . it's spooky,* he thought. It was difficult to embrace the vastness of the space, made up of artificially illuminated darkness and unpleasant fuel odors.

Noticing his son's discomfort, Mr. Yates tried to divert Daniel's attention by pointing up and away to the high bulkheads, the metal walls surrounding them. At the tops were catwalks, grated passageways that allowed a bird's-eye view of the entire room. They also provided another access to equipment higher up, such as control panels and electrical boxes, and were a way to get from one side of the ship to the other without climbing over the enormous engines.

"Let's go up there!" Mr. Yates shouted in order to be heard by his son, whose mind seemed lost. *There sure are some brave men working around here,* Daniel thought. They walked above a flurry of men weaving quickly and purposefully around enormous cylinders and generators, intricate circuit boards, and bundles of electrical cables. Everything seemed to be color-coded but mostly green.

"Where is the boiler room, Dad?"

"It's in a separate space. There is so much heat in there, probably reaching 140 degrees Fahrenheit, that workers need to wear protective gear to enter it. We can't see it from here."

The father and son walked around the perimeter of the enormous elevated surface. Daniel noticed how steady he felt in the "bowels" of the vessel. *One good thing about this place—these guys probably don't get seasick.*

Although he realized that the catwalk tour was a valuable experience, Daniel was eager to leave the heights and explore below. He remembered his dad stating that a ship was the most complicated thing ever built by humans, and he was anxious to get his hands dirty, so to speak, by learning about its internal functions.

They headed to the office reserved for the chief engineer. "Welcome," the Italian-looking man said as he removed his right glove and shook their hands. "So you've come to meet the Black Gang," he added with a smirk, a reference to the stokers in the days of the *Titanic* who would spend the entire day wheeling barrels of coal to feed the ravenous furnaces. "Don't worry, we use diesel fuel nowadays, so we don't get all black with coal—just oily." The officer handed them each a gray pair of overalls, clean but heavily stained.

Mr. Yates told his son, "Officer Magagnini is second in command to Captain Calamai. He keeps track of the machinery's performance and directs its maintenance. He also oversees other engineers and the whole function of this power plant."

Daniel found this fact remarkable and admirable. Perhaps he would rather consider a career as a chief engineer instead of a naval architect and marine engineer? He dismissed that thought quickly, though; he would miss the fresh air. Besides, he wondered if these men got as much appreciation. *They're mostly invisible,* he said to himself.

The engine-room tour was fascinating. Escorted the entire time by the chief engineer, Daniel learned about its various functions. He got an overview of the numerous areas before visiting them, knowing that the noise level would make conversation impossible.

"The boiler room generates steam for hotel services. Then there is the generator room, housing the turbo generators that provide electrical power. The main engine room houses the turbines that give us moving power. Last is an auxiliary area where the diesel generators are located."

They wound their way around machinery that blasted a cacophony of sounds—pounding, grinding, slapping, hissing, throbbing from many unidentifiable sources. Daniel and his father were handed protective earphones.

Along the way, Officer Magagnini shouted to introduce other men working the shift. "Each engine space has first, second, and third engineers on duty during any given shift. This is one of my first officers, Officer Cordera."

Arriving at a quieter area, Daniel asked, "Where are the watertight compartments?" His father had shown him how ships were divided into compartments, partitions that would contain and limit the spread of flooding if they were penetrated and water could get in from the outside.

Officer Magagnini replied, "We're actually standing in one of them. It's a bit of a journey getting to other compartments. They're made up of several walls and decks. But I'll tell you the ship has twelve watertight compartments, and it will stay afloat even if two of them are severely damaged."

Daniel, not wanting to seem disrespectful of the proud officer, thought to himself, *That's not enough! My ideal vessel will have more watertight compartments, even if it costs a lot more to build.*

By now, Daniel's curiosity seemed satisfied—and his ears had taken more than enough. *It's a good thing they wear ear protectors,* he thought.

Just as they turned around by a large circuitry board, the chief engineer, always aware of his men's whereabouts, thought he noticed rapid movement on the catwalks. He called the second engineer. "Who's running above the air-conditioning units?" he asked with urgency. Before receiving a reply, he noticed small legs dressed in Bermuda shorts scurrying behind the railings. "Who in heavens . . . *che pazzesca!* What madness!" the officer exclaimed.

Daniel recognized him. *It's that kid who got in trouble during the lifeboat drill, Darlene's brother.*

"I'll go catch him!" he offered.

"No. It's dangerous to chase the boy. If he trips . . . I'll call the captain and report this." The officer walked to the phone to make the rather unusual call.

By now, several men had seen this unbelievable act of daring. Some watched stupefied, and others prepared to chase Patrick.

Captain Calamai responded, "That must be the crazy youngster who delayed our voyage from New York Harbor last month. He'll do anything for attention."

Daniel felt somewhat uncomfortable hearing this, realizing that Patrick's sister and mother seemed like good, nice people and would be upset by yet another act of youthful mutiny. *Should I tell the family that the boy could be putting himself in danger?*

"How did he find this place?" Daniel asked the others, bewildered. They all quickly realized that the boy must have followed the Yateses from the pool, down the crew-only stairwell, and into the engine room.

Officer Magagnini shook his head in disbelief but did not comment. He was anxious to finish the Yateses' tour of his domain, as the captain would expect of him. After all, Mr. Yates's company, ABS, was always checking ships to make sure that they could be recommended to Lloyds of London for insurance.

The final thing, and perhaps one of the most important elements, that Officer Magagnini wanted to show Daniel was the emergency generator. They walked to an exterior bulkhead.

Daniel, wanting to appear knowledgeable, remarked, "Dad told me about this baby. It's supposed to kick in for emergency electricity. It might be needed for backup lighting, communication, alarms, fire equipment, and even to close watertight doors. And of course, it would provide power for lowering the lifeboats if they were needed."

Mr. Yates beamed with pride as he looked at his son, so young and so motivated. He knew that the engine-room visit would be only one of many explorations in the coming days onboard.

Officer Magagnini looked at his watch. Noting that the emergency generator was scheduled to be turned on at sundown, he took the liberty of asking Daniel to do so manually, even though it was twenty-two minutes early.

This hands-on experience became the clincher for Daniel. He now knew, beyond a doubt, what he was destined for. He couldn't wait to visit other parts of the ship. Each would feed him ideas for a new, better ship design. His passengers would be able to travel safely—under any circumstances!

"Everybody to the Pool!"

— *Friday, July 20* —

Piera

I was really excited about going to the pool today. Nonna finally said I could, after days of saying no. She told me she had packed my bathing suit in our carry-on bag, much to my surprise.

But then I remembered how my mother had written that the *Andrea Doria* was the first ship to have a pool for each class, including Third Class. She had written many letters during the last year. She told us that we would become a "blended family." She had married a Detroiter, and they had a baby born in August 1955. I was really looking forward to having a sibling.

My mother had also said that we would watch TV in our own living room, without having to go to the town tavern like before. She said we would have a family car, a violet Rambler station wagon. We also wouldn't have to kill our own animals for food; there were big stores called Wrigley's, and they had meat in small packages. I hoped she had a bicycle for me. I had learned to ride on her silver bike on Pranzalito's dirt roads, and I still had tiny pebbles embedded in my knees to prove it!

Besides, Patrick's relatives had bought him a new bike, and it was onboard. His sister, Darlene, had one. I should have one, too.

As we were finishing a warm breakfast of omelets, toast, a dairy food called yogurt, and a sugary spread named jelly, Patrick, in his shorts and T-shirt, flew by our table.

"Come on! Everybody to the pool!"

I guess he meant our table, but heads from every table looked up, probably wondering if it was an official announcement.

Nearby, Mrs. Dunes and her daughter, Mariana, stood up, ready to go. "Patrick's right. Come on, let's go to the pool," Mrs. Dunes said firmly, as if no one had a choice—especially Nonna. Mrs. Dunes addressed her: "Mariana and I will teach Piera how to swim. And don't worry, *Signora,* we won't let anything happen to her."

My Nonnis and I went to our cabin, where I put on a green and white bathing suit. My mother had sent it to me along with a full butterfly skirt, a frilly white blouse, a lace hat, and several pairs of shoes.

We met at the pool again, but this time it was different: I was in my bathing suit and looking as skinny as a rail. The Marinos were already there, as were the Hendersons and the Holmeses; in fact, there wasn't a spot on deck without a body lying on it. I imagined that all of Third Class had come to the pool. Children were giggling and running. American music was playing. It was really funny-sounding, not the pretty songs Nonna liked to sing along with. She cringed at this music, which everybody called rock 'n' roll.

Athletic Mrs. Dunes was already plunging in headfirst. I knew I would be learning to do that one day! Earlier, she had told us that she was considered a professional swimmer and gave lessons back in Naples. Today she beamed as she said, "I can also run eight-hundred-meter races."

Little Mariana had a plastic tube around her waist, and her mom was holding her around the stomach while she waved her arms and legs.

"After, I'll do the same with you, Piera," Mrs. Dunes said, seeing my interest.

Meanwhile, I had to use the bathroom. Up to now, I had always expected Nonna to accompany me. Today I wanted to show that I could leave her side and go by myself, like the Henderson children—and Patrick. It was just around the corner. I opened the door and felt a little uncomfortable closing it behind me, but I knew this was what everybody did. When I was done, I tried to open the door. It wouldn't open. I tried and tried, jiggling the knob and pushing against the door. Nothing.

I called out, "Nonna!" Then I pounded on the metal, thinking that no one could hear me. It felt as if there was no way out, except maybe by the thick rope descending through a circular hole in the floor that landed on the level below. *Me, climb down a rope? What if it goes down to the ocean?*

Horrible thoughts ran through my mind. Everything horrific that had happened in my last nine years played like a movie in front of my mind's eye. Getting my tonsils cut out while wide awake! Backing up into a scythe, barefoot, and cutting my ankle tendons! Hiding in a cupboard across town thinking that my great-aunt and uncle had come to take me to America! Getting stuck among the gears of an abandoned mill! Was today going to top my history of mishaps?

"*Aiuto!* Help!" I screamed, pounding harder and harder, thinking, *I'm going to die by myself in here. I'm going to fall into the ocean!*

After an eternity of probably two minutes, the door opened on its own. I stared into a sea of smiling faces. Everyone was happy about my liberation.

Nonna, teary-eyed, grabbed my hand and pointed out some people I should thank. "Patrick heard you first. Darlene came with him to help you. And Mr. . . ." She didn't know the man's name and waited for him to fill it in. Seeing that he wasn't going to, she said, "This nice man figured out how to unlock the door."

The "nice man" smiled. It was Mr. Murphy, Ernest Murphy, whom we saw regularly in the dining room and at the chapel, never uttering a word except while praying. He smiled at me nervously, rubbed his hands a few times, then walked away with quick, stumbling steps. With a slightly hunched back, he wound his way through the crowd while everyone still stared at me. Some people whispered as they turned their heads toward Mr. Murphy.

Nonna led me back to the lounge chairs, where she figured I'd rest from the ordeal, but I had another idea. I wanted to learn how to swim. Surviving the fright of the bathroom with a rope leading to the ocean had prepared me for other forms of survival, such as the swimming pool. Besides, all of my friends from the dining room were jumping in and out: the three Henderson children; the Holmes boys, except for the two-month-old twins, of course; and my youngest new friend, Mariana Dunes.

Mrs. Dunes kept her promise. There I was, floating with a rubber ring around my waist, just like Mariana! I looked at my Nonnis for approval. They wore nervous smiles, and I noticed that they looked as if they were dressed for church compared with the other families in casual clothes.

I felt even more accomplished when Darlene clapped. *My mom will be proud of me, too! I'll teach my baby sister to swim,* I planned in my mind.

I was becoming fond of Darlene, and she seemed to like me,

too. But I was surprised when she suggested that we go to the Reading Room together after swimming. *What will we read?* I wondered. *Do they have magazines and books in Italian?*

There was just one more thing. Would my Nonnis allow me out of their sight? I gave it a try. "Nonno, can I go read with Darlene?"

"You can bring books to the pool," Nonno replied.

Darlene made her case: "*Signora,* the Reading Room doesn't allow their books at the pool. It would be good for Piera to look at English books. I'll teach her some new words."

Nonna spoke up. "We promised her mother to bring her safely to America. If something goes wrong, she'll never forgive us!"

"Nothing will go wrong while she's reading, *Signora,* I promise!" Darlene's charm made Nonna smile.

"Don't let her out of your sight!" she said.

I jumped up and down, surprised that I wasn't scared to leave my Nonnis. I was suddenly concerned about *them! I hope nothing happens to them while I'm away!*

⚜

The Reading Room was quiet except for a lot of whispering. With people looking and pointing, it seemed that the hushed topic was Mr. Murphy. He was curled up in a modern-looking chair, dressed handsomely in his usual crisp white shirt, with an envelope in his pocket, the one he always had. And he was reading a book called *Moby-Dick* that he had brought to the pool earlier. I thought it must be really interesting, because it was big and heavy, with lots of pages.

Mr. Murphy wore thick glasses, which I assumed was from reading too much. I recalled when my friend Assunta in Pranzalito got to wear glasses. She looked so smart! For weeks, I pretended to be mildly blind so that my Nonnis would get me glasses. I even rubbed my eyes so pages would look blurred, but they didn't buy my act.

Besides being curious about Mr. Murphy, there was something else I wanted to know. It seemed like the right time to ask Darlene, "Why does Patrick have a bike on the ship?"

She giggled. "My aunts and uncles chipped in and bought him a beige bike with red stripes. See, 'cause my uncle in Italy, the butcher, his customers came to buy meat on their bikes. My brother took off for rides on their bikes every day. Zowie, did he get in trouble! So, at the pier, they surprised him with a new bike worth $150. Don't tell him I told you, but he really cried when a crew guy took it. He said, 'I'll put it in the garage.' I thought it was a swell idea, but not my brother!"

While I was engrossed in the bike story, something astounding happened. Darlene's brother, Patrick, walked in carrying a load of magazines under his arm. Actually, he strutted in, reminding me of how peacocks in my village showed off their long, colorful feathers. Patrick spread out the magazines on the table right in front of Mr. Murphy. The man raised his buried head, looked down, looked at Patrick—and smiled! It was the first time his lips had moved from a straight position except in prayer in the chapel.

"The two best things in my life are on this ship: my bike and *Dennis the Menace* comics!" Patrick declared to Mr. Murphy with the pride of a hunter returned from the hunt with food for a hungry family. "My favorite books of all—comic books. My uncle bought them for me in Italy, but they're in English." Patrick didn't seem to care that Mr. Murphy didn't speak; he would apparently speak for both of them. "You wanna read them?" he asked.

Mr. Murphy laid down the huge *Moby-Dick* and picked up one of the comic books. There were drawings on the cover. *That boy looks just like Patrick,* I noted immediately. The resemblance was almost shocking. *Could it be that the books are about Patrick?* The boy had unruly blond hair with a big cowlick, just like Patrick's. He had freckles like his and the same kind of smudges on his clothes. And his eyes were wide open, with a devilish look in them—just like Patrick's!

I didn't know what the title *Dennis the Menace* meant, but it didn't matter, since Patrick was quick to explain to his one-man audience, "He's my hero! He makes this boring world of big people fun. 'Never a dull moment' is his motto. He likes to stir up trouble! This guy"—he said, pointing hard—"he loves peanut butter just like me, he hates carrots just like me . . ."

At this point, I was lost. Darlene translated for me. She even told me what peanut butter was. "Lots of peanuts made into a spread to put on bread; it's an American thing." I immediately planned to ask my mother to buy some in Detroit.

But what fascinated me most was how Darlene played with her hair as she talked. While she was thinking, she twisted it around her index finger. When she was done thinking, she flipped her head really hard to make it unwind. Then she would talk for a long time, using words like "cool," "way out," or "zowie."

"Don't mind my brother," she said, snickering. "He's going through a phase of making mischief. That's why he likes *Dennis the Menace* comics. Unfortunately, every time he reads another comic book, he learns some new stupid thing to make my parents crazy . . ." She was ready to continue but stopped when I asked her what Mr. Murphy was reading.

"*Moby-Dick*. We read a short version of it in my English class." She twirled more curls on her head. "It was written a hundred years ago. It's about a sailor from Nantucket who did something wrong in his past. He goes to sea not even caring if he dies because he feels guilty. And the boat's captain, Ahab, is a crazy man who wants to kill a whale named Moby-Dick . . ."

Before she could finish, Patrick, who was listening to his sister's rambling while Mr. Murphy was thumbing through

73

Dennis the Menace, interrupted. "Yeah, but tell her why he wants to kill the stupid sperm whale. It bit off the captain's leg during a fishing trip!"

"Shhh," Darlene said loudly. "People are reading. And you're scaring Piera."

She must have noticed that I was stunned. All kinds of thoughts were racing through my mind. *Are there whales underneath this ship? Will they jump up and bite people's arms and legs off? Can they get into the pool? I hope Nonna doesn't hear about this!*

Patrick retorted, "She needs to get brave like Dennis the Menace."

Somehow this comment made me want to show him that I was brave. *Maybe that will stop him from scaring my Nonnis and me all the time!*

"Tell me more about the story," I asked Darlene, looking as if I liked what I was learning.

"Well, basically, the sailor, Ishmael, realizes his captain is crazy and . . . uhmm . . . he doesn't want to die anymore because a cannibal—you know, a guy that hunts for people's heads—teaches him that he can forgive himself for his past sins." Darlene saw my renewed fright and decided to bring the plot to a swift end. "And even though all of the fishermen die in the boat, sailor Ishmael—you know, the guy who wanted to die—survives when the whale rams the boat—"

"And the captain falls into the ocean and gets swallowed up by a lot of sea monsters," Patrick added with glee. "I read a comic book about it."

I made a horrible face, which prompted Darlene to take out another book—her diary. She touched my hand and said, "I want to share some secrets with you." Darlene seemed to understand that this was the only solution to get my mind off of ocean killings. "Do you want me to read you something I wrote?" She edged her chair closer and looked around to make sure that no one could hear. Then she began to read as she followed her writing with her index finger.

"Dear Diary,

"I can't wait to tell you about a really cute guy I met. Daniel. He's the dreamiest dreamboat ever! He was visiting from First Class. He dresses real sharp and seems just a little older than me. He's real smart and wants to build some really strong, unsinkable ship. I think he was kinda staring at me. I pretended not to notice. But I hope he comes back again. I gotta crush on him."

Darlene had written in English and was translating into Italian for me. *She's really sweet,* I thought, and I liked the sound of her low-pitched but giggly voice.

"Later, my brother told me he followed Daniel and his father to the engine room. He said, 'I'm gonna learn my way around

75

this boat so I can find my bike.'

"*But he got in trouble coming back up the stairs; a crewman ambushed him, he said. He thinks they all have a crazy plan to ambush him. I won't tell my mom. This is between siblings. I give him a hard time in front of people, but we're really best friends. I'm really proud of him learning all about the ship, even how to get to Second and First Class. He said they look nicer than our class.*

"*Hmmm . . . I might ask him to deliver a note to Daniel. Thanks, Diary, for listening.*"

So, Darlene and her brother were keeping secrets. *I wonder if she told him she has a crush on Daniel. Secrets are fun!* I decided that this was what I would do with my new baby sister. *But why is Darlene writing this down? Won't her mother find the diary?*

༺ஐ༻

After a nap in the cabin, Nonna looked at the ship program. "Piera, there's a dance in the Social Hall tonight," she said with the excitement of a little girl, or maybe she was trying to get me excited. "A band is going to play for us."

I was happy for her newfound joy but knew that Nonno would not want to dance. If he came, he would sit and watch—and look as if he were sitting on nails.

"I'm going to go ask Nonno to come with us," I said, running to his cabin. He was already dressed in his muted brown plaid suit. His white shirt was crisp, and his tie of tiny paisleys looked sharp with it. As I grabbed his hand and tugged, he reached for his fedora hat and his ever-present briefcase.

When we entered the big hall, the music was playing one of my favorite songs, "*O Sole Mio.*" I liked the words about the sun always shining except at night. I began to hum but stopped abruptly when I spotted Darlene.

She was dancing with Daniel!

She beamed as she looked at him. She must have put on her best dress. Its layers of light blue caught reflections of the twirling mirrored ball hanging from the ceiling. Little satin bows were sewn on the skirt part; the top was simple, with tiny straps adorned with a pearl necklace. Her hair was pinned up in a new style called a "beehive" that she had told me about. The back of her head held a big bow, like the miniature ones on her skirt.

I want to dress like that when I'm bigger. Darlene looks beautiful! And Daniel likes her; he keeps talking and staring at her face. I wonder if his parents know that he's here with us. Will they dance all night? Are they going to get married one day? I was so excited for my new friend that all kinds of thoughts danced in my mind.

Life onboard was opening up new portholes to a world I had never known. I liked the view, with new spaces that filled my mind.

Remembering the Titanic

— Friday, July 20 —

First Class

The lifeboat drill was haunting Daniel. He asked his father if they could return to the boat deck, and he agreed. They walked down the glass-lined teak corridor, where they could look up at the modern, untouched lifeboats suspended above the deck windows. Mr. Yates walked silently with his hands behind his back, waiting for Daniel to initiate a dialogue.

Realizing that his son's silence meant that Daniel was grappling with his thoughts, Mr. Yates said, "Son, I take it you weren't pleased with the lifeboat drill."

"I guess I was disappointed, Dad," he replied. "The *Titanic* tragedy was supposed to teach us to take the drills seriously, so why were there no directions . . . and why didn't the crew show up in full force?"

"You're right, son. The *Titanic* tragedy brought about changes that we must be grateful for—specifically, a mandatory lifeboat drill and enough lifeboat space for every passenger." The naval architect looked pensive and added, "I'll have to address this with Captain Calamai." He added, "Is that what's troubling you, Daniel?"

Daniel nervously rubbed his hand over his sleek crewcut. "Actually, when I returned to our stateroom, I remembered some scenes from the movie *A Night to Remember*. Too many questions were left unanswered . . . at least, in my mind." The young man searched for the right questions. "Why did people wait so long to board the lifeboats? They knew the ship had hit an iceberg! And why weren't there enough lifeboats for everyone?" His voice had escalated with each question.

Mr. Yates knew that it was the right moment, as a father and a scientist, to confront the details of the tragic event of forty-four years earlier.

"Do you recall reading testimony given by the *Titanic's* owner, Bruce Ismay?"

Daniel nodded.

"Mr. Ismay said that the ship was looked upon as being a lifeboat in herself. He also said that the builders had only provided lifeboats to pick up a crew from another ship or in case of fire onboard."

"Yes, Dad. But when Ismay was pressed to answer, 'Did you

not consider having them for the purpose of saving the crew and passengers?' he responded, 'No, I do not think so.'" Daniel felt anger growing as his face tightened to prepare another difficult question. "So why didn't the British Board of Trade provide enough lifeboats for everyone?"

"That's a tough question, Daniel. Perhaps they didn't know how to design a ship with more lifeboats without filling up the decks, or maybe they thought it would be unnecessary . . . or too costly."

Daniel now felt rage flowing through his veins. "Too costly? There were human beings onboard." He hesitated, then unleashed another angry bout. "Maybe they assumed that only steerage passengers would be the dead ones!"

"Now, son," Mr. Yates said, placing his arm around Daniel's shoulders, hoping to calm him. "I agree that there was unfair class distinction and too many poor immigrants died. But things are different now. There are enough lifeboats for all passengers on the *Doria,* plus more than two hundred extra lifeboat spaces."

He looked into his son's eyes and knew, with complete certainty, that Daniel's compassion for others would lead him to design safe ships. But he was unsure, for now, how to lessen his son's anger regarding the ethics, or lack of them, during the *Titanic* tragedy. He awkwardly tried to help.

"Is there anything else that you find troublesome about the *Titanic?*"

"Yes, there is," Daniel said, loudly enough for passersby to hear. "Why did Bruce Ismay break the law of the sea? Why was he so cowardly?'

Mr. Yates cleared his throat and pointed to the empty bench. They both sat and looked out at the calm, innocent-seeming body of water. The scientist continued. "I know that history has labeled Mr. Ismay as a coward, but I'd like to give him the benefit of the doubt, son. We weren't there to know all of the circumstances. Maybe there was room in some lifeboats because of the reluctance of passengers to board. They were not aware of the ship designer's dire prediction that the ship would sink in one to one and a half hours. Mr. Ismay probably did know of the ship designer's dire forecast and perhaps panicked."

The father did not mind elaborating, seeing that this was an opportune time for examining the human conscience— especially one's own.

"Remember, son, Ismay told a steward who was uncovering a lifeboat, 'There is no time to lose.' There is even speculation that it was Ismay who ordered, 'Get the women and children first into the lifeboats.' A steward did tell Captain Smith that it was he, and Smith ordered, 'Go ahead; carry on.'"

Daniel felt a bit more reassured that Ismay might have been caught in hopeless circumstances, and it could even be that he actually acted honorably.

Mr. Yates hoped to temper his son's judgment of people

facing insurmountable odds. He added, "Also, consider that initially, both men and women hesitated to board the lifeboats, thinking that the larger boat was safer. One passenger said that an officer gave him a push and said, 'Here, you big fellow, get into the boat.' Undoubtedly, Mr. Ismay had, like all of us, a sense of self-preservation. He may have taken the officer's words to apply to himself." He paused and then continued, "One real tragedy is that Thomas Andrews was allowed to go down with the ship. As the designer, he had critical information that could have been useful to science."

Daniel had always admired his father's moral judgment. Maybe, just maybe, his father was making sense about Ismay, the supposed coward.

He waited silently as his father hesitated before concluding, "Self-preservation is a very strong sense. How we think we would act and how we actually act when in the throes of survival are two very different things."

Daniel was beginning to see people's actions in the *Titanic* tragedy differently. He wondered how he would have acted had he been in Ismay's position. Then he looked straight into his father's eyes and asked, "Dad, how would you have acted in Ismay's place?"

The father-teacher-scientist replied without hesitation, "During any life-threatening events, I would do my best to show the utmost courage, even if it meant death. I would do whatever I could to help my fellow man—this is imperative for survival during sea accidents. If I were to die, you and the family would know that I did my best to survive but faced death honorably. If I did survive, I could walk down the street with my head held up high." He concluded, "You'll just have to design an indestructible ship, so that people are not faced with gut-wrenching sea survival."

The naval-architect-to-be smiled, then lightheartedly suggested, "Let's go see what Mom and Margaret are up to." Writing his technical report on the *Andrea Doria* lifeboats would have to wait. Besides, that day's discussion with his father was more important than scientific details.

Storm!

— *Saturday, July 21* —

Piera

Even though it was cloudy and rainy outside, Darlene said that this was going to be a special day.

"Tonight I'm going to be a contestant in the Miss Teen Eleganza fashion show with other girls," she said, giggling with a hint of modesty. "The boys and their fathers are gonna have some fun, too. They're judging the contest in the Social Hall. One of us will get a trophy. I hope it's me!"

Darlene had invited me to the Reading Room after lunch, telling my Nonnis that she would teach me more English so I could talk to my mom. Secretly, I was hoping that she wanted to read me another page of her diary. Because the sky was dark, most of our friends had decided to read instead of going to the pool as usual.

I looked around the room for familiar faces. Mr. Murphy was nervously flipping pages, with his head buried in *Moby-Dick*. Mrs. Dunes and little Mariana were reading some kind of farm book and making animal noises. Mrs. Henderson sat on a couch reading while her flock of three went through one book after another. *Where's Patrick?* I wondered. *I wish he'd bring back his comic books for Mr. Murphy.*

I was eager to learn new words, but Darlene seemed too excited to teach. She kept looking at her red-painted nails as she talked. She couldn't twirl her hair in her fingers because she was wearing a polka-dot scarf.

"Is that why you have pins in your hair—for the contest, I mean?" I asked her.

"Yeah. I want to make sure my flip holds its curl onstage and when we walk around the tables. The boys and the men will be judging everything: our clothes, hair, smiles, and how we walk. And . . ." She wiggled her whole body in the chair, held her breath, then released it with, "I invited Daniel!"

"Can I come?" I was very happy for my friend and wanted to be a part of her world. I wanted to learn how to be just like her for America.

"Golly. Of course! Everybody is invited, but I want you to be there for sure."

"What will you wear?"

Just as she began her reply, we felt the ship swaying to one side.

"Oh, dear! I'd better teach you a few English words before the storm comes, or your grandma will have you under her wings for the rest of the day."

"What storm?" I asked, worried.

"Don't worry. This happens at sea. The ship will sway to one side, then the other, because of the big waves. Just pray we don't get seasick, OK?"

"What's 'seasick'?"

"It's when—"

The ship swooped upward and slowly came down again. Darlene laughed as she held her stomach. I knew we were in for rough sailing—and possibly throwing up our lunch. My stomach started feeling queasy.

"OK. Come on. Learn these words. Daniel taught them to me on a piece of paper."

I repeated each word after her, along with its meaning. I tried to sound American as I said, "Starboard side: the right side of the ship. Port side: the left side of the ship."

Darlene chuckled as we rode the next tilt to starboard, and she said, "Starboard! Whoooo!

"Here are two more words. Bow: the front of the ship. Stern: the back of the ship."

As I repeated, she congratulated me. "*Brava,* Piera!"

I knew that my mother was going to be very proud of me. Just as the word "stern" came out of my mouth, Nonna flew into the room howling, holding her stomach, and saying, "I knew I shouldn't have let you out of my sight! It's a disaster every time!" She was talking about the day before, when I panicked and couldn't unlatch the bathroom door.

"Nonna, I'm not scared! It's just a sea storm with big—"

My grandmother waved a swift good-bye to Darlene. As she pulled me from the chair, she declared, "We're going to our cabin and be close to your Nonno."

As we were fleeing from the Reading Room, the storm became more dramatic. Nonna held on to a table by the exit door, holding me under her other arm as we swayed from side to side and up and down. As if creating more drama to scare Nonna, our friends made a spectacle for us. Mrs. Henderson lay on the couch while her eight-year-old, Ilene, lost her balance and fell right on top of her expectant belly. Mrs. Dunes dropped her cup of coffee, which spilled on the farm book, making Mariana cry.

And poor Mr. Murphy. He looked like a frozen statue, just as he had during the lifeboat drill. He looked at the ceiling as if the storm was upstairs and was coming down to possess him. He clutched *Moby-Dick* to his chest for comfort, but it didn't seem to help. His hand rubbing became compulsive after he laid down his book. He slapped his whole hand over his pocket as if he was worried about the envelope he always had there.

Oh, the poor man, I thought. *I wish Patrick was here to*

comfort him. Or Sister Angelica. Why can't the captain do something about the rocking ship?

To make matters worse, a waiter lost hold of a tray he was carrying over his shoulder. Cups, saucers, coffee, pastries, and ice buckets all smashed to the floor.

All of this was just a teaser for what was to follow. The giant liner began acting like a toy sailboat in a tsunami. As it continued its forward motion, it rolled more violently and pitched down and up gradually. As it rolled from one side to the other, some of the furniture that was not fastened down began to slide into a pile. This was repeated about every ten to fifteen seconds. Each time, the pile of wood and cushions grew larger. At one point, we grabbed and hid behind large pillars for protection.

Between each roll, crew members grabbed some of us and asked us to seek shelter in the passageways for more safety. This also protected us from some of the windows that were exploding. Fortunately, they were interior windows, or else we might have been slammed by waves.

With each forward dip, my grandmother hollered, "Oh, *Dio!* We're heading to the ocean floor!" Mrs. Henderson and Mrs. Dunes gave her a cross look each time, but she was oblivious as she made the sign of the cross after each holler.

Nonna and I huddled together for comfort. I felt like crying but didn't want to seem cowardly in front of the other children. *If poor Mr. Murphy doesn't cry, I won't, either. I wish Nonna would be more brave. Is Nonno being brave—wherever he is?*

After a couple of hours of this tormenting adventure, there seemed to be a lull. Darlene ran out of the room, holding her stomach with one hand and cupping the other over her mouth.

Nonna and I hurriedly wound our way down the stairs. The rolling movement beneath our feet made us rock from one wall of the stairwell to the other, and Nonna synchronized her shrieks with each swell. My stomach matched the swells with heaves.

As we tried to move downward, we met face-to-face with Mrs. Marino. "Have you seen Darlene and Patrick?" she asked. For the first time, she wore fear instead of a jovial smile.

We told her that Darlene had been in the Reading Room bathroom but that we hadn't seen Patrick. Nonna pressed on with me in tow.

We reached Nonno's cabin at last. He looked really scared, sitting on his bed and holding on to the post.

Poor Nonno; he's too old to be so scared. I no longer thought about my own fear as we all sat on the bed together, me between my Nonnis. It was at this point that I made an observation about the two people I loved most in my whole life: they never touched each other. Their only physical bond was through me. In our farmhouse bedroom, I had slept with Nonna, while Nonno slept in his own bed next to ours. *I wish Nonno would hug Nonna. She needs it.* I was worried for them.

As the waves splashed violently against the porthole, they

looked foamy white against the black clouds. This new sight was enough to provoke Nonna into a long lamentation.

"Why did we leave our village, our friends? We probably won't make it to America. We're going to drown on this God-forsaken ocean!" Then she used God's name in vain, which made me feel uncomfortable.

I don't like myself when Nonna says these things. I feel as if I'm a big sacrifice. My reflections were making matters worse. I ran into the bathroom and threw up for a long time.

When I returned, I noticed Nonno's briefcase rolling in and out from under his bed. The curtains were swaying, and the bathroom door slammed shut, precipitating a jump and a scream from Nonna.

Although the swells seemed to be getting smaller, Nonna didn't seem to care. She continued her sobbing and shrieking with each rocking movement.

Maybe we shouldn't be on this voyage to America. It's too hard! My seasickness was worsened by a heavy dose of guilt.

Finally, Nonna's wails diminished as she lay down and rode out the storm's finale.

⁂

"I'm hungry!" I announced, to my Nonnis' amazement.

They didn't object to moving out from our small comfort zone of the cabin, and we didn't struggle to walk this time as we headed for the dining room. Everyone else must have been hungry, too, because they were all at their assigned seats.

Mrs. Marino caught our attention as she was talking to all of the tables around her about her son's latest adventure on the high seas. "The crewman was so mad when he brought Patrick to our cabin! He was holding him up by his sweater and stretching it."

I looked at Patrick. He was sitting quietly and seemingly humiliated, very unlike his usual "I can get away with anything" attitude. I thought he might cry at any minute.

His mother said, "The crewman was actually Captain Calamai's first officer! He said, '*Signora,* we found your son hiding behind a Rolls-Royce in the garage during the storm. He could have been seriously hurt if the car had shifted. I brought him to the captain, who is very upset by your son's mischievous behavior. He asked that he remain in your company.'"

Now Patrick actually did have tears plopping onto his cheeks. "I was just making sure my bike was OK, Ma."

"Did you see your bike?" Darlene asked excitedly, still wearing her polka-dot scarf covering bobby-pin curls.

"No, dopey. The crewman yanked me out of there. I could have found—"

"Don't be sassy with your sister, or I'll ground you. It would make the captain and the crew real happy. Wait till your father hears about this!"

I spied the three nuns and the two priests smirking, as were

Mrs. Henderson and her three children. *Poor Patrick! No bike, and now he's punished, too. I wonder if his mother will make him attend the fashion show.*

All of a sudden, I realized that Mr. Murphy wasn't in the dining room. *He must have gotten scared to death. I wish he'd join Sister Angelica.* I was truly worried about the man.

After the awful sea storm, everyone seemed ready to cast their cares overboard and become friends with the sea again. The "pool gang," which was also the "dining-room gang," went to A Deck in full force to support Darlene in the fashion show. "Miss Teen Eleganza" was going to be chosen by an all-male panel. The crew had put together a stage, strung lights, and attached some stairs for the ten girls.

I was so excited. This evening was going to be about my best friend onboard, Darlene. And I knew she was very excited, too. "This could be the first step of my future career," she had told me earlier. Now I could hear her giggling with other girls in a room near the deck. *I really hope she wins! She's going to be a fashion designer—she has to win.* I was rooting for her with every fiber of my body.

My Nonnis were now wearing their most calm expressions of the voyage. Maybe they felt as if Mrs. Holmes's terrible omen had been lifted. During the rolling and swaying of the storm, Mrs. Holmes had had an awful premonition: "I kept seeing my babies, the twins, in a cradle floating on dark waters, and they were out of my reach!" Nonna had gasped so deeply upon hearing this at dinner that she inhaled some bread and started choking.

But now people's smiles seemed to say, "Reality is stronger than omens, and we deserve to enjoy the moment."

The audience was filled with families like the Holmeses, the Hendersons, and the Duneses and many single immigrants whom Nonno had met. Nonno looked casual in his beige shirt, with no jacket for a change. But he clutched his briefcase on his lap.

I heard clapping. As I looked around wondering why, I saw Daniel. He looked extremely handsome in a sport jacket—the only one in the audience wearing one. I realized he probably wanted to impress Darlene.

There was more clapping. Ten girls paraded out in a line headed for the stage. *Wow! They look gorgeous! Darlene is definitely the prettiest.* In my mind, she had already won the trophy.

A woman got onstage and introduced herself as Loretta, a boutique owner. She would be describing the girls' dresses for us. As she spoke, the judges' panel of three teenage boys and their fathers were reading from a piece of paper and admiring four trophies on the table.

The first girl, Giovanna, stepped forward to a swooning Italian song called "Heart and Soul." The boutique lady smiled wide as she said, "A perfect prom dress. Covered in pink roses with long green stems, in a crisp sheer organza over layers in soft pink. A fitted bodice with velvet olive-green trim at the waist that ties in a bow at the back."

Francesca was the second model. It was difficult to focus on her red dress, covered with glitter called sequins, because her ankles kept twisting. Her lips quivered when she tried to smile. I heard someone whisper, "Stage fright."

All the while, the judges were whispering to one another, not seeming to notice much onstage, and looking confused about what to do.

Loretta went on with Annika, the next model. "Annika's dress is of bold black velvet with a sheer chiffon white layered hemline, a fitted bodice and full prom skirt, with floral corsage details on the skirt and clear rhinestones."

Then Darlene was introduced. I heard "oohs" and "ahs" as she smiled, looked down at Daniel, and twirled twice. She seemed to be both walking and dancing to *"O Sole Mio,"* which was now blasting from the loudspeaker.

I'm glad she kept bobby pins and rollers in her head all day. Her "flip" looks perfect. I was admiring every detail, including Darlene's shiny red lips.

The boutique lady seemed to like her dress a lot. She said it was "fanciful and romantic," which I didn't understand exactly. I just liked that it was the fullest of all the dresses.

My friend kept twirling to Loretta's words. "Darlene looks beautiful in a champagne-colored, shimmery organza fabric layered over tulle and taffeta, strapless, with a full tea-length skirt consisting of a swagged organza layer, a gathered tulle layer, and a taffeta layer beneath."

I looked over at Mrs. Marino and Patrick. Darlene's mother was clapping and beaming with watery eyes. Patrick, wondering about all the commotion, made the effort of lifting his embarrassed face, which had been buried in his arms on the table. He quickly resumed the head-down "victim" position.

I looked around, clapping hard, hoping that everyone else was doing the same, and was surprised to see Sister Angelica and Mr. Murphy also clapping. I hadn't even seen them come on deck. *Thank God, Sister Angelica found him! Maybe he locked himself in his cabin during the storm.* I was relieved to see the nervous soul smiling and clapping, the first such gesture I had seen from him.

Daniel was smiling and clapping, too, but he was being sophisticated about it. He acted as if he didn't want to draw attention to himself, keeping the focus on Darlene. She beamed at her admirer.

The rest of the girls shared their fashion flair as the judges looked up nervously from their ballots. *Can't they pick the right girls?* I wondered. *The boutique lady should help them.*

With a swoop of her arm, Loretta introduced each one so we could clap some more. Then she asked for the results.

"And for the best smile, the trophy goes to Annika." Annika

grinned widely as the moon's glow reflected a beam off her very white teeth.

"The best comportment goes to Giovanna." I agreed that she had looked very mature.

"And for the best hair and makeup to enhance the dress, the prize goes to Constanza!" I agreed again, since her black "bob" held by a red headband looked elegant with her long red nails.

"Our judges bestow the trophy for the girl with the prettiest dress to . . ." There was a short hesitation, as if the boutique lady forgot what to say. But she fooled us. She shouted, "Darlene!"

I shrieked with joy! I was really proud of her. She looked so beautiful in that dress, which she had designed and made herself.

Several of us stayed on deck to congratulate the judges and the girls. But Darlene disappeared quickly. Then I saw her mother staring somewhere toward the very back of the deck— the "stern," as Darlene had taught me it was called. Darlene and Daniel were standing side-by-side. Darlene was laughing as she kicked her foot up backward. Daniel just kept talking, with his arm wrapped around the back of her waist.

Patrick didn't notice anything. His face was still hidden. Then something amazing happened. Mr. Murphy approached Patrick, laid a hand on his shoulder, and muttered something. "Ccc- . . . cccommm- . . . bbbbkkkk."

Sister Angelica translated for Patrick, who was now staring up at Mr. Murphy. "He says he wants to see your comic books again."

Storm Stories

— *Saturday, July 21* —

First Class

First Class passengers had been warned by crew members that the ship would be experiencing parts of the hurricane that had bypassed Bermuda. It was now headed into the Atlantic. Passengers asked one another, "What will this do to the ship?" The crew's vague replies created less comfort than desired.

Daniel and his father had been enjoying beautiful skies on the glass-lined Promenade Deck when the storm clouds rolled in. Mr. Yates wanted to seize this opportunity to teach his son about storm waves. He only had moments to do so. The crew was announcing that the sightseeing deck would shortly be closed.

"Why don't they want us out here?" Daniel asked.

"For a couple of reasons," his father replied. "The lounge

chairs are going to be removed to protect passengers and windows. And of course, the crew is afraid that people will overreact as they see the waves growing in height."

"How tall will the waves get, Dad?"

"It depends on how many thousands of miles they've been traveling to pick up speed. Conservatively, they'll reach twenty-five feet, but they could possibly grow to forty-five feet. If they get any taller than that, they'll be monster waves. Mariners called them rogue waves."

As they spoke, dark gray storm clouds filled the sky. The ship began rolling from side to side. Quickly, Mr. Yates pointed out, "Look how fast the waves are traveling. The higher the wind speed, the higher the waves. So that wind must be really gusting. Do you notice how the ship is responding with an increasing roll and pitch?"

Daniel and his father leaned against the interior wall for a moment before making a dash to the ship's interior.

"Do scientists know at what point people start getting seasick?"

"That's a good question, son. Yes, they do. But first let me tell you that people get seasick because of vertical motions. The faster the bodies are taken up and down, the more likely they are to feel discomfort. If people's bodies move up or down in less than one-tenth of a second, then surely there's discomfort."

"Actually, now I remember reading that this is one of the

reasons that the *Titanic* had a dummy smokestack—to create stability and reduce rolling."

A crewman suddenly yelled down the corridor at the Yateses. "Quickly, move inside! The Promenade Deck is off-limits!"

As Daniel and his father wound their way down the stairwell, the ship rolled more violently. The forward and backward tilt made them feel as if they were trying to walk on stairs in a house of horrors. *I hope Darlene and her family are doing OK,* Daniel thought.

Some diners had lined up at the windows to watch the spectacle created by the waves. As they reported what they saw, others began to take flight for their staterooms. Waiters who had just laid the entrées on the tables were quickly removing them. They carried trays piled high. Some flew out of their grasp and smashed in the aisles. The crashing noise and fear of flying dishes had more people rushing for exit doors.

"Your mother and sister must be in their staterooms," Mr. Yates said.

"I think we'd better help Mrs. Ascoli," Daniel offered. "We don't want her to smash her fingers or lose her jewels." He pointed toward the elderly pianist. It was said that she had recently picked up her inherited fortune in Italy.

Although Daniel had been joking, he realized that the old woman was becoming hysterical.

"Help me! Help me! I need to get to the safe. I need to get

my jewels!" Daniel and his father approached the frail lady and offered words of comfort. It didn't seem to help that the ship's bow was now plunging into large oncoming waves. Each plunge downward was accompanied by a loud noise from the wave slamming.

"When is this storm going to calm down?" the old woman asked.

❧

The lull after the storm drew First Class passengers to the elegant dining room, where the clinking of fine china and delicate crystal chimed along with the cheerful chitchat. It was the fifth day of the passage to New York. The ladies were wearing their fifth spectacular gowns. Many had been packed in a "trunk closet," complete with hangers so they wouldn't wrinkle.

The Yates and Campi families sat engaged in conversation. Mr. Yates asked the Campis how they had weathered the first storm. Mr. Campi looked perplexed at the word "first." And the naval architect said, "I simply assumed this was your first storm at sea."

Daniel interjected with a chuckle, "This certainly wasn't Dad's first storm adventure. Tell them about the *Queen Mary,* Dad." As everyone looked at Mr. Yates, the scientist began to explain with a hint of shyness.

"Well, let's see. It was in February of '37. I was returning to the States on the RMS *Queen Mary*. We were approaching the shoals of Nantucket. Around midday, the seas began to get choppy. I had lunch in the First Class Dining Room and took a stroll on deck. I wanted to challenge myself in predicting the severity of the storm by studying the wave heights and the time between swells. Two gentlemen I had met earlier saw me and suggested that I follow them to the Third Class swimming pool. It had been closed, but people were watching the pool water, mesmerized. It had begun to move with the ship's motion to a point where two different surges coming from opposite ends of the pool met at midpoint and created a large water spout that reached the canopy overhead. Each time, we got doused but still enjoyed watching this phenomenon—a kind of wave study."

At this point, Daniel became impatient and said, "Dad, aren't you going to tell them about your stormy date?"

This prompted a stare from Mrs. Yates.

Margaret pried. "Come on, Dad. Tell us, did you have a date?"

The prim and proper gentleman blushed. "Yes, a woman from Third Class. But first let me finish from where I left off. Since the Third Class pool was too turbulent for swimming, the crew told people that they could use the First Class pool. It was smaller and several decks lower in the ship. Wave conditions at around one o'clock were not too bad; they reached about twenty-five feet high. The ship, however, maintained her forward speed with occasional wave slamming."

"Isn't that called a 'bone in the teeth'?" Daniel asked, showing off his knowledge of nautical lingo.

"Yes, son!" His father chuckled and quickly continued. "Around four o'clock, I went swimming in the First Class pool, and although there were some surges of water, it was safe enough to swim. Also swimming was a lovely lady from Third Class. I wanted to get to know her but wasn't really comfortable with the swaying of the ship. I asked her if she would like to meet me later in the First Class Smoking Room. She agreed. As I headed up to A Deck, I noticed that the decks were deserted as the wind was gusting at about seventy knots. Walking up the stairs was tricky because of the undulating ship. It was actually going from rocking back and forth to lurching side-to-side— almost like when you swirl a brandy."

Eight-year-old Julie Campi exclaimed, "That's what happened when we were going up the stairs to our stateroom during the storm today! Mommy was tossed off her feet, but Lisa grabbed her by her blouse. It felt like I was in a horror house where the floor and walls move!"

Everyone smiled, and the naval architect continued his saga. "For some strange reason, I decided to dress and go to the dining room for my evening meal. Only about ten people were as crazy as I was. Waiters were having problems carrying their trays. A wine steward lost a tray full of glasses and wine bottles, and a dining steward dropped his tray of empty dishes. The ship was hitting forty-five-foot waves at a speed of twenty-six knots."

"What about your date, Dad?" Margaret implored.

Mr. Yates grinned and continued. "Just for the record, in '37, I hadn't met your mother yet. After dinner, I went to meet my date, Ivana, in the Smoking Room on the Veranda Deck. It was the highest space on the ship for passengers—don't ask me why we were so foolhardy. Ivana lit a cigarette, and we were sipping cognac. Then she casually asked me what the white object was that was passing across the windows to starboard. It was dark, but you could make out the whitecaps of breaking waves. I told her, 'You do not want to know what that was!' It was a forty-five-foot swell!"

At this point, the three girls looked at one another and pretended to bite hard on their fingernails.

The marine scientist ignored them and went on. "The ship's forward speed had slowed to about six knots to contend with the storm and the waves."

Daniel inquired with authority, "Didn't the captain extend the fin stabilizers, Dad?"

Mr. Yates explained, "Daniel is referring to systems designed to reduce the effects of waves or wind gusts. Yes, the fin stabilizers were extended, but it wasn't enough to save Ivana from disaster. As I looked from the window back to her, she was on an abrupt backward plunge—chair and all. She had overturned one hundred eighty degrees to port. On her back, she tried to find her way out of the pile of skirt fabric that was covering her. When she finally stood up, she rubbed the back of her head, said good night, and dashed out.

Mrs. Yates asked, "Was she hurt, darling?"

"No, I don't think so, but her ego was bruised. I didn't see her at the pool anymore. But the excitement didn't end there. Upon seeing Ivana's mishap, a woman at the bar at the forward end of the Smoking Room yelled, 'It's another *Titanic!*' Instantly, passengers started yelling and running. I stood up and shouted, 'Silence!' I told them that the ship was in a bad storm and that this would be over within hours—which did happen. Someone asked, 'Who's he?' I told them I was a naval architect. The room quieted down."

Mr. Yates's audience looked absorbed in his adventure of nineteen years earlier.

Daniel asked, "Were there announcements from the bridge during the storm?"

"No, son, but you make a good point. A simple explanation would have calmed a lot of frayed nerves. Passengers want to know that the bridge has everything under control. I did visit the captain the next day with a fellow passenger, who told him, 'This young naval architect served you well. He quelled the effects of the storm in the room.'

"The captain thanked me and asked where I had studied. I told him I had graduated from the University of Michigan only two years before. The whole thing was quite an experience for a green naval architect."

Mrs. Yates said, "Daniel wants to follow in his father's footsteps and attend the University of Michigan's School of Naval Architecture and Marine Engineering when he finishes high school next year."

Mr. Campi said that he was happy to have acquired more dramatic experiences to include in his *New York Times* article, adding, "And today's storm will be included, too."

"Look, Daddy, isn't that the captain?" Julie asked, excited to see the tall, stately ship master in a black uniform passing near their table.

Captain Calamai was more comfortable on his quiet bridge than among the sociable passengers. Yet after storms, he wanted them to feel his presence, as a way of reassuring them for the remainder of their passage. Mr. Gibson, president of the New England Bank, gestured with a wave to invite the captain to his table. He introduced his wife and four children.

Margaret Yates said, "I hope he comes to our table. I want to invite him to dine with us tomorrow night for my birthday." The captain caught Mr. Yates's welcoming smile and proceeded to their table. As he circled, shaking hands, he arrived at Margaret, who asked, "Captain, will you join us for dinner tomorrow evening? We're going to celebrate my fifteenth birthday."

"Thank you for the invitation," Captain Calamai said. "I will make a note of it, but I must assess sea conditions before leaving the bridge." Then he added with a playful smile, "Duty first."

As the captain moved on in the role of principal host, Lisa Campi asked, "Who wants to go to the horse races?" It was instantly decided that the girls would soon be betting their nickels on wooden horses, and Mr. Gibson's daughter, Betty, would join them.

Daniel asked his parents to excuse him from the evening's events. He wanted to get down to Third Class before the fashion show started.

❦

Shortly after dessert, the First Class passengers made their ways to several decks, according to which events listed in the ship bulletin they wanted to attend.

Mr. and Mrs. Gibson sat mesmerized as they watched two professional dancers exhibiting the sensuous moves of the Argentine tango. They would soon be indulging in group instruction from the "Dance Lady."

Their teenage sons were at their favorite spot atop the ship: the Belvedere Lounge. As throngs of teens and adults danced to "Only You," they chatted, hoping to find fun dance partners for a "fast dance."

Mr. and Mrs. Yates, sitting at the lido bar, enjoyed a spontaneous serenade by fellow passengers who sang and played the mandolin. The most popular requests were "*O Sole Mio*" and "*Arrivederci, Roma.*"

Margaret, Lisa, Julie, and Betty shouted for their favorite "horses." There were many prizes for all game participants: trophies, certificates, cups, and prints of the beautiful *Andrea Doria.*

Julie was winning the race when people suddenly started heading for the stairwell. Word was spreading with tsunami speed that an Italian circus was performing in the Social Hall. Many wondered why it had not appeared on the daily ship bulletin. Perhaps it was a last-minute decision by the troupe, or perhaps the staff had only just hired them to divert people's minds from memories of the day's storm.

Performers tossed rings while standing on one another's shoulders. A monkey strummed a guitar to accompany dancers. Ladders were brought out for animals to climb and show off clever tricks at the top, such as juggling oranges.

The room was packed, people clapped, and dancers at the back erupted into the can-can. It was planned pandemonium.

The clock struck midnight—time for the nighttime buffet, along with more activities and adventures. Only those suffering from seasickness chose to visit the ship hospital instead of indulging in the fun.

Protection from Fear

— *Sunday, July 22* —

Piera

As we approached the chapel on the Foyer Deck, the sweet smell of incense drew us into a sacred space. My Nonnis seemed quite ready to participate in this act of gratitude for surviving yesterday's big storm. They walked quickly and with purpose on each side of me.

The back row of pews was taken up with figures in black. Sister Angelica and the two other nuns, along with Fathers Kennedy and Gardner, were kneeling and praying, sometimes burying their faces in their hands.

I noted that Mr. Murphy was not with them. *I hope he's coming to this service.*

We chose a pew near the center, where we could watch the

door and see everyone who entered. *Who are all these people I've never met?*

My question was answered when Nonna whispered to Nonno, "*Guarda tutti i ricchi!*" She wanted him to notice all the rich people from First Class joining us. Mrs. Henderson had told us that this was the only place where we would see passengers from Second and First Class. She told us to look out for movie stars from Hollywood.

"Nonna, will you tell me when a movie star shows up?" I asked.

She didn't reply, choosing to pull out her crystal rosary, probably because she didn't want to admit that she would not recognize a movie star.

I thought I could identify the passengers who traveled in the other classes by the way they dressed, held their heads, and walked. Something about "them" was different from "us." The women wore a lot of pearls, and many had flowers in their hats. "Our" people wore simple lace veils to show respect in the Lord's home. Some elegant ladies wore lace gloves and held patent-leather purses on folded arms. Their shoes were of the same color and shine, and all of them had high heels. They all looked serious and self-absorbed.

"Nonna, is that a movie star?" I whispered as a lady entered in a white mink stole, three rows of pearls, short wavy blond hair, and shiny red lipstick. She was the first blond lady I had ever seen!

"I think so," she whispered between her Ave Marias, while continuing to stare at the door.

As I studied the kneeling worshipers, I almost shouted to my Nonnis, "Mr. Murphy is here!" Instead, I pointed to him, with his shiny bald spot, rubbing his hands as he prayed.

He was sitting near the Marinos. He and Patrick seemed to have developed some kind of bond. Darlene looked pretty in a white cotton sailor dress trimmed in blue to match her blue beret with a red ribbon.

The congregation stirred as the clock struck ten, and Chaplain Natta entered with folded hands. We stood in unison.

After some prayers at the altar, the chaplain asked us to sit. The sermon he had prepared had something to do with how people should act when they're scared. "Preservation of life is very strong, but we must act unselfishly toward our fellow man even when we fear dying," he said. He asked us if we'd thought about how fearful our fellow passengers were during the storm the day before and what we did to help them.

I wish we had helped Mr. Murphy! He was more scared than we were.

The chaplain told us that storms and accidents at sea are God's way of testing our faith, of giving us opportunities to be strong and to help our fellow man. He quoted the Bible about courage. "Yesterday was a trial of courage," he said.

Nonna cleared her throat.

"The Lord believes in redemption," Chaplain Natta continued. "He expects you to confess your sins, improve your actions, serve your fellow man as you would serve the Lord."

I recalled going to confession in Pranzalito before making my First Communion. In the dark booth, where I could see someone stirring behind the holes in the wooden slats, I confessed that I had not helped my friend Domenica when she twisted her wrist. Instead, I had run home in fear as she cried. The priest gave me ten Ave Marias and ten Lord's Prayers to say to redeem myself, and he made me promise to be braver when others were crying.

Chaplain Natta even gave us a personal example. "My courage was tested on the high seas. I survived two accidents. I learned to show compassion even when facing death. We must be humane."

There was a very loud cough, like when someone is choking. It came from Mr. Murphy. The poor man's face had turned an odd purplish color and was covered by shiny beads of sweat. *Oh, I hope he's not sick!* I said a prayer for him as I watched him rubbing his hands together over and over.

Fortunately, Chaplain Natta led the small congregation into song, and the loud coughing was no longer heard. It was the song for communion, "O Lord I Am Not Worthy." It was sung in Latin and then in English. As we watched a few people go to receive the sacrament at the altar, I remembered that my First

Communion dress was onboard. That made me very happy. It was the prettiest dress I had ever seen, and almost everyone in Pranzalito had secretly told me that it was the prettiest one out of all the dresses on all the girls from all the towns that day.

I felt like a bride wearing it. It had a very poufy skirt. The top layer had eyelet lace flowers throughout; these even covered the poufy arms. The entire bottom was scalloped in lace. A tulle veil crowned my head. But what I loved the most, I think, was the doll purse that was dressed to look just like me, the seamstress's special creation. *I can't wait to show the dress and the purse to my mother!*

While I was thinking about my dress, I was also thinking about how loudly Mr. Murphy was singing. *He got over his cough—and he can talk!*

Chaplain Natta told us to take a prayer card from the pew pocket before we left. The prayer, "Our Lady, Star of the Sea," was about being protected from danger on the high seas.

❧

After relishing a delicious lunch, our group dispersed in all directions. The Holmeses announced that they were going to the pool to enjoy swimming lessons from Laura Dunes. The nuns headed for the library, and the priests were going to learn fencing.

Nonno announced that he would be learning to play shuffleboard with other immigrants. "It looks like bocce ball, so I think

I can handle it," he said.

Darlene asked Nonna if we could return to the Reading Room. "*Signora,* the skies are blue. There won't be any more storms. I promise!"

Nonna surprised me by agreeing, saying that she would check on us during her card game.

My heart jumped for joy, thinking that Darlene might read her diary to me.

When we reached the Reading Room, now a familiar space, Darlene asked, "Do you want to learn more English words or hear my diary?" I pointed to the diary, trying to conceal the smirk growing on my face. "I thought so," she said, laughing.

For the first time, I noticed a sweet fragrance on her. She must have noticed my quick sniffs.

"Cologne . . . or eau de toilette, as they say in French," Darlene said. "Let me quickly read to you about last night before your grandmother comes back."

I sat in awe of this young woman who entrusted me with her secrets.

"Dear Diary,

"Wait till you hear about last night—the best time of my life! I got to show off one of my creations in a Paris-style fashion show. I can't believe the judges liked my dress the best! Mom had said the fabric was really expensive for a young lady my

age. But she spoils me that way 'cause she knows I dream of becoming a famous fashion designer.

"What a swell idea to invite Daniel! He got to see me looking beautiful. You won't believe this: Daniel gave me a sweet, short kiss on the lips. I was on Cloud 9, 'cause Daniel is so cool! Jeepers, I think my crush is getting bigger!!!

"I can't wait till I see him again. He asked me for another date (Ping-Pong or the library). Zowie! This is gettin' serious!"

Darlene blushed as she read. She followed the writing with her fingers, and I noticed a lot of exclamation marks. "I'm soooooo excited about the rest of this trip!" she exclaimed.

Then we saw a familiar sight: Patrick and Mr. Murphy reading *Dennis the Menace* comic books together. Darlene and I covered our mouths and laughed. "I bet those comics are really different from *Moby-Dick!*" I said with a giggle.

Thanks to Darlene, I was learning more than words like "propellers" and "turbines." I was also learning about life and about living away from Pranzalito.

When I get to America, I'm going to ask my mother for a diary so I can write about everything I'm living.

A Gala Dinner

— *Sunday, July 22* —

First Class

Excitement and revelry were brewing in the First Class dining room. It was to be a Gala Dinner night, one of two during the 101st voyage of the floating wonder of Italy. Ladies, gentlemen, and their families entered the elegant room in their finest apparel in anticipation of an elaborate dining extravaganza.

The women all wore long gowns with layer upon layer of lace, taffeta, organza, or silk. The skirts were made even wider in contrast with the tight-fitting waistlines, torsos, and busts. The strapless bust lines held their perfect contour by means of hidden wires. A few ladies wore sheer shawls on their shoulders to create additional flow of form. Most preferred not to wear necklaces, opting for long-stranded earrings that sometimes brushed their shoulders. Others added corsages to their wrists, bought at boutiques onboard.

Men with elegant women on their arms walked taller than usual in their black tuxedos, some with tails, and bow ties.

The younger people, also dressed up for a gala night, had been reminded to be especially polite. They walked slower than usual and watched their parents for approval.

Everyone was smiling.

The Yateses and the Campis sat together at their assigned table. Margaret Yates and Lisa Campi asked to sit together. Their parents liked the idea. The girls had become pals, and it was also Margaret's fifteenth birthday.

Lisa had decided that her flowing pink dress, coming to just below her knees, would be perfect. She was fond of the lace straps that matched the full skirt. Margaret had declared white to be her official birthday color, thinking that it would contrast beautifully with the colorful party balloons.

Having not lived in the States for two years, Margaret had asked her parents for a "real American-style birthday." Her mother had talked to the chef, and a surprise was brewing.

Mr. Campi, always in his journalist role, began the table conversation with a charming smile. "So, Daniel, how was your visit below? Do I remember that you were headed down to Third Class and the engine room?"

Daniel, seeming quite comfortable in his black tuxedo

and burgundy bow tie, replied, "We met some fine people in both places."

The reporter prodded. "What's it like in Third Class? Is it adorned with art everywhere like here?" He glanced at the paintings and bas-reliefs on the walls.

The murals depicted an allegorical street scene—it was like strolling in an art museum devoted to Italian culture. Lisa Campi, who loved to study art, had explained the day before, "This work represents how a ship is built around an artwork. The finest muralist of Italy, Salvatore Fiume, was commissioned to invite passengers to become part of the metaphorical city. We get to stroll under porticos and strike up conversations with illustrious people: Napoleon and Josephine, Galileo, dukes and duchesses."

Mr. Campi had passed on his own love for Italian art to his daughters. They knew the works of Michelangelo, Giotto, Raphael, and Leonardo. The Campis had chosen to travel on the *Andrea Doria* so that their daughters would be immersed in its art. But at this moment, his question about shipboard art was not appreciated.

"Papa," Lisa interjected, "it's Margaret's birthday, and we want to have fun!"

Her mother, Josephine, agreed. "Darling, why don't you interview Daniel and Mr. Yates tomorrow in the lounge?"

Mrs. Yates sat back in relief. She had spent hours making sure that the birthday celebration would be extra special for Margaret.

Mr. Yates was pleased, too, as he raised his glass of freshly poured spumante, an Italian sparkling wine, and toasted, "To Margaret!"

With orchestrated precision, the waiters, all in white tops and black pants, meandered around tables carrying bottles of spumante on silver trays over their shoulders. They moved in step to the spirited music of Verdi, Puccini, and Vivaldi.

Margaret looked up in delight as she recognized the movement "Summer" from Vivaldi's *Four Seasons*. "I play that piece on the violin!" she enthusiastically announced, "and I would love to try an arrangement on the piano if I ever locate one."

Mrs. Yates added, "This afternoon, Margaret and I attended a concert. The orchestra played one of her favorite works, the *William Tell* Overture."

"Then Mom scheduled a real surprise for me," Margaret said. "A fencing lesson in full attire. It was tricky looking through the screen covering my face!"

Everyone was delighted for the American birthday girl. It all seemed perfect, but Margaret still had a burning wish: "I wonder if the captain will join us for dinner."

"Look over there!" Mrs. Campi exclaimed. "It's that rich lady—you know, the elderly pianist who's supposedly bringing lots of precious jewels from Italy to the U.S. They're an inheritance from her mother. They say they're worth millions."

Those at the table turned to see what the lady was wearing.

Betty found humor in the wealthy woman's style. "All those diamonds! Gee whiz, I need my sunglasses." She giggled as she pulled a pair from her purse.

Margaret added, "And how about all those animal furs she's wearing! Scary!"

"Now, now, girls. It's not a bad thing to be rich. Let the woman enjoy it."

It was time to feast on the delights prepared by chefs who had been trained at the famous Cordon Bleu school in Paris. Colorful menus with flowers in Italian motifs on the covers adorned the tables. The Yateses and the Campis studied the elaborate gourmet offerings thoughtfully—except for Margaret. Her mother had arranged for the kitchen to prepare her favorite dish, lobster tails with mango butter, a specialty of her native New England.

Margaret sat with her hands folded, looking around at the walls and admiring the eighteen panels of inlaid wood depicting eighteen different architectural structures. Lisa had told her that Ilario Rossi of Bologna had designed the floor-to-ceiling artwork.

Mrs. Campi put down her menu and remarked on the elegant china, all precisely placed. Numerous pieces of delicate crystal and elegant silverware, all designed by famous craftsmen, completed each place setting.

"There's a lot of gold on this table!" Mrs. Campi joked. "I wonder how much gold is on each plate, cup, and saucer?" The gold trim on the outer rim of each piece was enhanced by gold scrollwork an inch wide just below it, a gold crown from Italian royalty, and, under that in bold gold letters, "ITALIA."

When their waiter arrived, everyone was eager to order hors-d'oeuvre, but they looked to Margaret in agreement that she should start. "I'll have the eggs Moscovite." In her honor, they all ordered the same, along with the same soup, *minestra* Italian style.

But the entrées would be based on distinct individual cravings, including wild game, mutton, steaks, and seafood. And Margaret displayed her knack for cracking the lobster shell.

They all skipped the homemade pasta dishes, but no one wanted to miss the traditional salads and assorted cheeses that followed the entrées.

The youngest of the Campis, eight-year-old Julie, showed much more interest in the dessert menu. "I can't decide—the cream caramel, the pudding soufflé, or the English trifle," she said.

Her mother offered, "You've always enjoyed melted chocolate cake, honey. Why don't you stick with that so you won't be disappointed?"

Just then, a tall, handsome Italian waiter approached Margaret. He was carrying a giant cake lit with fifteen sparking candles. Margaret's eyes opened wide. In unison, the table broke out in song: "Happy birthday to you . . ." The excited young lady made a wish and blew out every candle, and everyone clapped. The waiter handed Margaret a long, fancy silver knife to cut the first piece of the multilayered cake, the layers divided by chocolate soufflé cream. He then treated the others to generous pieces as another waiter scooped out American vanilla ice cream.

"Thank you, everybody!" Margaret said jubilantly.

And then her mother took a gift-wrapped package from under her chair and placed it in front of her.

"Here you are, honey. Enjoy!" Mrs. Yates said. Margaret tore it open to discover a book, *Profiles in Courage* by John Fitzgerald Kennedy. "You know, it's a best seller, and it might win the Pulitzer Prize!" she added. "Luckily, they carry it in the ship bookstore."

Margaret was thrilled. She was fascinated by the most-talked-about couple, Jackie and John Kennedy, but also she enjoyed reading as many best sellers as she could get her hands on.

Her father added, "Since Margaret spends a lot of time crossing oceans, she prefers books about the sea, but she'll like this one just fine. Besides, we wouldn't want to inundate her!" He chuckled at his own play on words. "She's already read *The Caine Mutiny, The Cruel Sea, The Old Man and the Sea,* and *A Night to Remember* about the *Titanic.* This young lady can handle a lot of daring adventure!"

Dinner was not yet over. It was customary to refresh the palate with fruits, whether dried, in syrup, baked, or drenched with a coulis, and always accompanied by platters of fine nuts and dates.

Around the dining room, people pushed back from their tables in collective agreement: Life was perfect on the *Andrea Doria.*

"Look! There's a hand coming out from under that table!" someone exclaimed. As everyone turned to the pastry table with its ice sculptures, they saw a small hand reaching up from under the pleated tablecloth. Then a small head appeared and looked around, like a small animal checking out its surroundings before running off.

Daniel walked across the room, reached under the table, and pulled out Patrick. He had recognized him as Darlene's brother and didn't want to cause him trouble, but he realized that he was being watched. With his back to the room, Daniel winked at Patrick but spoke in a stern voice. "Young man, you need to go back to Tourist Class"—as Third Class was also called—"or I'll report you to the captain!"

A few people applauded, and Daniel welcomed the appreciation. He watched the boy run off—with pastries bulging from his pockets.

Daniel returned to his table and looked at his father for a reaction; Mr. Yates patted his son on the back.

Then another family came over and began shaking hands. It was the Gibsons from Nantucket, with their three teenage sons and nine-year-old daughter, Betty. Mr. Gibson had asked his employer, the New England Bank, for a long holiday; he wanted to treat his family to a European tour in a large rented van. The three families had met in the lounge the day before, and the children had all gotten acquainted.

Mr. Gibson said, "Why don't you all join us for a stroll to the Belvedere Lounge? When it gets late, the kids can keep dancing to Latin rhythms and that crazy new rock 'n' roll. We older folks can have nightcaps in the lido and watch the moon. The music goes on until the wee hours of the morning."

Betty Gibson, who preferred the company of animals, asked, "Can we go visit the dogs first?"

Her mother, who had brought her to pet the dogs in cages on the top deck during daytime, replied, "No, dear. The dogs are sleeping now. We can see them in the morning."

Everyone looked at Margaret, wanting the birthday girl to finish the day as she wished. "Let's go dancing!" she exclaimed.

Mr. Campi said, "Show us the way to the top of the ship!"

Mr. Murphy's Mishap

— Monday, July 23 —

Piera

What upsetting news! My pool friends and I were stunned to learn that Mr. Murphy was in the ship hospital. Mr. Holmes had just returned from visiting him there and was telling us about it.

Mr. Murphy had really tugged at our heartstrings. He seemed especially fond of the younger folks on the ship. And he'd rescued me from a bathroom tragedy!

I looked at Patrick, who had made friends with the stammering, shy old man. He abruptly stopped making animal noises and came to stand beside his mother.

"Why is he in the hospital?" Patrick asked Mr. Holmes.

"Don't worry, young man. He'll be all right. He hurt his ankle during the night."

We all felt bad, but Patrick reacted immediately. He disappeared like a flash of lightning.

Mrs. Henderson asked Mr. Holmes a few questions, but he replied, "I'm sorry. I don't know the details, and I need to go help my wife with the children." We understood—the five Holmes youngsters were a handful.

My Nonnis looked concerned, and Nonna held me tight, as if sheltering me from the news.

I wish we could go visit Mr. Murphy.

Patrick soon returned, holding a *Dennis the Menace* comic book. "Can we go visit Mr. Murphy, Ma? I gotta give this to him."

The menace himself brought a big smile to our faces. It seemed the devil boy who had caused a lot of heartburn among adults now wanted to bring goodwill to one of them.

Maybe I can bring the old man something, too, I thought.

"Sure, son. That's a great idea," Patrick's mother said.

She and Darlene and my Nonnis and I followed Patrick up the stairs to the hospital on the Foyer Deck. *How in the world does he know where he's going?*

Patrick's mother seemed proud, saying, "My son has gotten around this ship, hasn't he? I think he could draw a map of it by heart."

We went into a room with curtains hanging from the ceiling and beds behind them. The nurse, who introduced herself as Antonia, welcomed us warmly and escorted us to the last curtain.

Mr. Murphy met us with the biggest smile I had ever seen in my life. His eyes got bigger and bigger as he looked at each one of us and nodded. *I think he's got tears in his eyes—I think it's because we're here.*

Dr. Tortori invited us to approach his patient. As we did, Mr. Murphy became even more emotional; he tried to talk. "Ttttt- . . . tannnnn . . . youuuu," he uttered, taking a big swallow, his neck and body seeming tight.

Nonna said, "Listen to that! He talked for us!" She wiped away a tear.

Patrick, who had been staring at Mr. Murphy's blue, swollen ankle with a bone looking ready to pop out, exclaimed, "I had an ankle like this when I fell out of a tree!" He looked at the patient and asked, "Did you break it?" The old man nodded. Patrick moved closer and said, "Don't worry. It will get better," and he handed Mr. Murphy one of his handy tools in dealing with adults: a *Dennis the Menace* comic book.

"Tttttt- . . ."

"Don't mention it." Patrick swayed from one foot to the other, hands in his pockets.

Mrs. Marino and Darlene were beaming. Darlene gave Patrick a little hug. *She's proud of her brother—she told me so in her diary.*

Nonna nudged me; she pulled some pieces of hard candy from her purse and pointed her head toward the patient, who was groaning a little in pain. I was happy to give Mr. Murphy my humble present and watch him smile again—between groans.

Dr. Tortori said it was time for another pain pill and that his patient would be asleep soon. "He'll be as good as new in a couple of months if he stays off his feet," he said, looking at Mr. Murphy as if giving him a warning.

We all waved at our friend and hoped that he wouldn't have to walk anywhere for weeks.

As we thanked Dr. Tortori for letting us visit, I noticed a wrinkled envelope in his pocket. It was the one that Mr. Murphy always carried in *his* pocket, and it had been opened.

Nurse Antonia was answering Mrs. Marino's question about how the accident happened.

"Well, his cabin mate told us that he believes Mr. Murphy was trying to sleepwalk. During the night, while he was trying to get out of his bed, he landed with a big thud on his right ankle. He also said that Mr. Murphy was shivering and yelling, 'Don't just leave them there!'"

What could he have been dreaming about? I wondered.

"When will he be able to get out of bed?" Nonna asked.

"Oh, certainly not during this voyage," Nurse Antonia replied.

On the way to our cabins, Darlene had asked me if I wanted to see something "really different." Nonno brought me to the Game Room to meet her. While we waited for Darlene, we stood by the Ping-Pong table and watched four young men bat the ball back and forth for a long time before it went astray. Then they laughed a lot, joking in a different language: "*Wunderbahr! Nein! Achtung!*" Nonno reminded me that they were German.

Darlene arrived carrying a small wicker chest. Nonno asked her to watch out for me at all times. She smiled and said, "*Certo, Signore*. Of course, sir."

Nonno waved and left. I wanted to ask him where he was going but didn't want him and Darlene to think that I was worried—really, I was just curious.

"Did you ever play with paper dolls?" Darlene asked me as she pulled some wooden doll forms out of the chest.

"No. In Italy, I made a doll out of an ear of corn. I painted eyes on it from berry juices and wrapped it in rags for clothes."

My friend pulled her head back, surprised, but quickly continued to describe her dolls. "These are for serious fashion designers, kinda like mannequins but flat. I design my clothing styles using these." Then she pulled out outfits of various colors and fabrics. "These are baseball outfits for girls." I looked at the white and purple pants and tops curiously. "Oh, golly, I forgot. You don't know about baseball. Well, it's a game with a ball and a stick that they play in the States. A guy hits a ball in a field, and the other team tries to catch it. The hitter runs on a grass diamond. People cheer to make him run faster. The ball gets thrown around, and the hitter is either safe or out."

Jeepers, I can't wait to play baseball. Oh, I'm using Darlene's favorite word! I'm starting to think in two languages! I was making some interesting discoveries about fashion, baseball, America—and myself!

Darlene continued, "When I get back to New York, I'll make you a green dress and mail it to you."

I squealed. "*Grazie!* Thank you!" Then I watched a fashion parade out and back into the wicker chest.

Will she tell me more about Daniel now?

Although I loved being with Darlene, I was anxious to get back to my Nonnis. It didn't even matter that she had said nothing about Daniel. The two of us walked out on deck repeating the new words she had just taught me: "bulkhead," "buoyancy," "berth." Daniel had taught her that sticking to one letter of the alphabet at a time would make the lesson easier.

"Look, Darlene. It's Daniel. He's running this way!" I said. Daniel was happy to see Darlene, not only because he liked her but also because he had something to tell her.

"Darlene, your brother's in trouble. He let a dog out of a cage. I need to talk to your mother . . . the captain . . ." he tried to explain while catching his breath.

Darlene and I were confused but understood that Patrick was capable of all kinds of antics. We walked toward the pool, where Mrs. Marino was reading her *Parade* magazine.

"Mom, Daniel wants to tell you something," Darlene began.

Patrick, suspecting something, was watching us from the poolside.

"*Signora,*" Daniel said politely, "your son did something . . . well, something he wasn't supposed to do." Patrick's mother shadowed her eyes with her hand and looked up suspiciously at Daniel and then at her son as Daniel continued. "He was in the Belvedere Lounge and opened a dog cage. He did some damage . . ."

Mrs. Marino didn't seem to care if it was the dog or Patrick that did the damage. She was furious.

"Get over here!" she ordered her son. Patrick strolled over like a shy, wobbling duck. "You're grounded for two days. You're not to leave my sight. It's for your own good—and everyone else's. You're putting yourself and the passengers in danger all over this ship. Everyone will see you as a good-for-nothing by the time we get to New York."

To escape her wrath, we walked away, and we looked back to see an officer approaching Mrs. Marino.

Ship Anatomy and the Racing Whippet

— *Monday, July 23* —

First Class

There were plenty of onboard activities for physical enjoyment, but tea hour in First Class satisfied the desire for communication and, often, intellectual stimulation. In the lounge, the white-uniformed waiters offered an assortment of teas to be individually chosen from red wooden boxes. The exotic aromas flowed from porcelain decorated with a Chinese motif designed exclusively for the First Class of the *Andrea Doria*. The passengers examined the pastries displayed on silver trays placed under their noses.

"I feel as if I'm back in London," Mr. Yates told Mr. Campi, with whom he had agreed to meet, along with Daniel, to provide material for the *New York Times* article.

"I'd love to visit London one day. Maybe we'll sail back to Europe on the *Andrea Doria* for our return trip to Spain," the journalist said.

Mr. Campi's suggestion led the marine scientist to quip, "You mean you're not discouraged after Saturday's storm?"

"Actually, the storm's going to add value to my article. I now have a real respect for Mother Nature's role in sea travel. Besides, we weathered the storm just fine." With his notebook in hand, he asked, "Do you mind if I start by asking you some questions about your ship investigation?"

"Please, feel free," Mr. Yates replied.

"Well, first of all, how does your company, ABS, fit into the picture?"

"Vessels have to be built according to ABS's Rules and Standards," Mr. Yates replied. "Then they give information about their construction and features to underwriters for insurance purposes. Lloyds of London is the *Doria's* insurer."

"I see," Mr. Campi said. "Can you give me some of the ship's basics?"

Here Daniel took over, eagerly rattling off facts. He told Mr. Campi that the *Andrea Doria* had a gross tonnage of 29,000 and was 697 feet long. "That's about the length of two football fields," he said. The ship's beam—"that's the width"—was 90 feet. She could do a maximum of 26 knots, or 48 kilometers per hour, but service speed was 23 knots, or 43 kilometers per hour. "She's propelled by two steam turbines attached to twin screws, and—"

"Wait, wait!" Daniel's father interjected, seeing that the reporter seemed overwhelmed with the young man's rapid recall. He realized that Mr. Campi was finding all of the technical data beyond his scope. "Daniel, you might want to slow down a little bit so Mr. Campi can take notes."

The reporter politely said that he wanted the details but that what interested him the most was the *Andrea Doria's* safety features.

"That's my favorite part about this ship," Daniel replied enthusiastically as he plunged into the topic. "There are enough lifeboats for more than two hundred people, the maximum number of passengers onboard—unlike the *Titanic!*"

Mr. Yates grinned and said, "Daniel is quite a *Titanic* enthusiast. If we don't stop him, you'll learn everything about that ship, too."

Daniel went on. "Let me back up. The *Andrea Doria* is considered the safest ever built! It meets all of the SOLAS 48 requirements."

"Sounds impressive, but what's SOLAS?" the journalist asked, flipping to a new page in his notebook.

Daniel spoke with more knowledge than Mr. Campi expected. "It stands for Safety of Life at Sea. The SOLAS Convention is considered the most important of all international treaties concerning the safety of merchant ships. It was passed in response to the *Titanic* tragedy, and it prescribes the number of lifeboats and other emergency equipment, along with safety procedures."

"Can you give me more examples of this?" Mr. Campi asked.

"Well, the *Doria* has a double hull. That means two exterior walls are used as a barrier against seawater in case the outer hull is damaged and leaks."

The reporter looked quite impressed as Daniel continued. "The *Doria's* structure is reinforced with bulkheads—that's walls—for twelve watertight compartments. They keep seawater contained if there are leaks. In fact, the *Doria* is a two-compartment ship. That means that as many as two watertight compartments can be damaged and the ship will still stay afloat."

The last remark troubled the journalist. "That's great. But what if there's a really high impact? Let's say three compart-ments get damaged. Then what?"

Mr. Yates clarified. "Naval architects don't anticipate that this will happen. There's no collision in history that's been documented to penetrate more than fifteen percent of the beam. That would mean thirteen and a half feet of the *Doria*. Can you imagine a ship ramming us at a high enough speed to penetrate more than that?"

Mr. Campi did not look comforted by this logic. Daniel decided that it was a good time to tell the journalist about his dream of building a super ship that would be nearly unsinkable.

"I see that you're concerned about this the way I am, Mr. Campi. That's why I want to build a ship with more watertight compartments and have it withstand even more water inflow before it sinks."

Daniel's father looked pleased but explained to his son why this was not practical. "Such a ship would have to be as big as a battleship. Imagine how hard it is to do maintenance when you have to walk around, over, or under more than a dozen compartments. Besides, having more compartments doesn't ensure safety. The *Titanic* had sixteen compartments, but they were flooded as its many thousands of rivets failed." The expert wanted his son and the journalist to hear the truth: "No ship is 'unsinkable,' unless it's filled with cork!" He chuckled. "Then there wouldn't be room for cargo or passengers."

Daniel looked worried. *What will this mean for my project? What features can I include in my super ship?*

His father continued, even though he saw disillusionment replace the enthusiasm on Daniel's face. "Italian naval architects wanted three-compartment flooding in their design. It was proposed, but they found that it wasn't possible because it would have added far too much cost."

Mr. Yates realized that it might be a good idea to lighten the topic with an anecdote about safety. "Look, you're not the only ones who are concerned about safety. Earlier, Daniel and

I were delayed unexpectedly in Third Class while touring the ship. You should've seen this poor old man during the lifeboat drill! He looked traumatized. We went up to him and asked if he needed help. But he was perspiring so heavily that he couldn't even see our faces. We asked him his name, and he began to stammer."

"It sounded like mmmrrr . . . mmmrrrfff . . ." Daniel said.

Mr. Yates, feeling awkward about Daniel's imitation, interrupted and added, "A man standing next to him said, 'Murphy, Ernest Murphy. He's my cabin mate."

Mr. Gibson, the New England Bank chairman, was sitting at the next table. When he heard the name Ernest Murphy, he turned to them and said, "I know who he is! I read about him taking a trip on an ocean liner so he could rid himself of his terrible fear of sea travel. I remember reading the article last month, because the man does business with my bank." The other gentlemen seemed interested, so the banker continued. "Murphy is a respected philanthropist. His focus is to fund organizations for children who have lost parents at sea—fishermen, passengers. I don't know all the details. I do know that he was headed for Ireland to meet with large charities, the Marine Society and the *Titanic* Relief Fund. Seems like a great guy— and a very modest man. And by an interesting coincidence, 'Murphy' means 'sea-battler' in Irish."

"That's probably why he's traveling in Third Class," Mr. Yates noted.

Daniel shared his own observation. "Mr. Murphy probably chose to return to the States on the *Doria* because of her safety measures and impeccable record." The men all nodded, their curiosity about the mysterious passenger seemingly satisfied.

As the banker turned back to his family, the journalist pursued more information. "OK. I'm convinced now. A lot of science has gone into the *Doria's* structure, and it's surely a safe vessel. Daniel, you mentioned her record. Can you give me some history on her voyages?"

"Sure. This is voyage one hundred one. Basically, the *Doria's* record is spotless—except for her maiden voyage."

Mr. Campi looked up from his notebook, wide-eyed and curious. Daniel proceeded. "She was traveling near Nantucket when she encountered a bad storm. A swell caught the ship broadside. She rolled twenty-eight degrees, so people couldn't stand anymore. People fell, and twenty were injured."

As Daniel finished his sentence, he noticed that an officer was beckoning to him, calling him to the other side of the lounge. He excused himself and went over to the officer.

"We found this ABS pin in the garage yesterday," the officer said, cupping the pin in his hand and passing it to Daniel. "Someone said you were wearing it earlier."

Daniel stood frozen, unable to speak. *Now the captain knows I was in the garage, where I wasn't supposed to be. I hope he'll still give me a recommendation for college!* Then he muttered, "Thank you."

Just then, interrupting the unpleasant news, Betty Gibson ran over and asked Mr. Yates and Mr. Campi, "Can I ask Margaret, Lisa, and Julie to go visit the dogs on the Belvedere Deck? Daddy said I could go."

With permission, Betty ran off to find the other girls.

A waiter arrived and offered the gentlemen some tea.

⚜

It was a lazy, breezy afternoon on the highest level of the ocean liner. On the Belvedere Deck—whose name in Italian meant "beautiful view"—passengers took in a breathless, borderless ocean panorama.

Betty wanted to show her ship pals her own special discovery: the canine passengers of the *Andrea Doria*.

The girls approached the six cages, which held three poodles, a Chihuahua, a shih tzu, and a whippet. Each day, the dogs were placed on the Belvedere Deck to enjoy the warm sun and cool breezes.

"Don't open that cage!" a waiter shouted at a young man who had been petting the white whippet. The girls watched a boy about Betty and Julie's age backing away from the cage as its door flew open.

"*Aiuto!* Help!" The waiter, seeing potential disaster, summoned other waiters as he hastily laid his loaded tray on a small table, watched it crash to the teak deck, and mumbled something under his breath.

Meanwhile, the boy took flight down the stairs, leaving the pandemonium to unravel behind him. The whippet, a breed known for racing ability and a dislike for cages, took off in his newly found freedom. He raced in a circle around the deck. He was unstoppable as he continued to lap the entire circumference over and over. Waiters and passengers tried to intercept him before he slipped into a photography shoot at one end.

It was too late. The blond model, who had been identified as a famous actress, began screaming. "My fox fur! Get the fur off that stupid dog!" The photographer, peering from under a black cover over his head and the camera, was shocked to see the dog holding the head of the fox in his mouth while the long brown fur stole covered his body. It looked as if the fox had come to life and was racing along with the white dog.

For several minutes, "the poor man's racehorse," as whippets were known, was happy to display his racing skills on an oval track—the Belvedere Deck.

By now, all of the passengers had risen to their feet to watch the "race." The actress's screams were followed by high-pitched wails of despair. "That stole's for my next film!" The dog was seeking his own fame while his caged buddies watched, the Chihuahua singing his praises with long, high-pitched howls.

But the unexpected hunt was not soon to be over. The whippet turned so quickly around one end of the deck that music from the jazz trio came to a halt as the drum set was invaded by four skinny, lanky legs that dragged the tripod cymbal stand. A cymbal whirled like a flying disk and crashed with a clunk.

By now, a crew member was calling for assistance. It was too late for the fox to win any race; the fur stole flew off the whippet's back, slid over the railing, and floated to the ocean. The movie star sat sobbing with her head buried in her hands.

The whippet, hearing the Chihuahua cheering him on, decided to stop and sniff around his cage just long enough to be intercepted by five waiters, who grabbed him and shoved him back into the cage. They hadn't noticed the owner, an elderly lady wearing a Chanel suit, and her son, in spats, approaching the cage.

"Who did this? Why wasn't anyone watching Wesley?" the elegant lady demanded.

The first waiter to arrive at the scene tried to repair the damages. "A boy was petting him. I don't know what made him unlatch the cage—*stupido!*"

His disdain for the boy's actions was not going to let the waiter off the hook. The elderly lady exclaimed, "The captain will hear about this! Wesley is on tour to race at prestigious events. If his legs are hurt . . ."

❧

Betty couldn't wait to tell her family about the excitement she had just witnessed. She ran down the stairs and described the event breathlessly. "Jeepers, you won't believe this! We, the other girls and I, saw a boy. He unlatched the whippet's cage. He ran off, and the whippet ran all over the place. He stole a lady's fox boa . . . ran all around dozens of times. Dogs were howling . . . people were laughing. His owners said something about injured legs . . . suing the captain . . ."

"OK, honey. Calm down first. Then tell me, what boy did this to the dog?" Mrs. Gibson asked.

"I never saw him before. He's about my age, I think. He had this little bunch of hair sticking straight up on top of his head."

Daniel Yates, still engaged in discussing the *Doria's* safety design, heard Betty's strange account. He thought, *This sounds like Darlene's brother. I'd better go warn her and her mother of what's to come.*

"I'd like to come back to this discussion tomorrow, if we can. It will give me time to rethink my project," Daniel proposed.

His father and Mr. Campi agreed and continued talking about more lighthearted topics.

"What I Learned"

— *Tuesday, July 24* —

Piera

Dear Diary,

Darlene told me to start writing to you. She said, "Feed your diary with secrets. Talk to it when there's nobody to talk to." So, I'm going to try.

I miss my cat, Carla, so much. I'll tell you things I can't tell my Nonnis—just like I did with Carla. I know they've enjoyed being like parents to me, but soon they have to give me up! It's so unfair! Should I live with my mother or with my grandparents? Who should I love more? I don't want to hurt anybody's feelings. Maybe we can all live together and love each other lots.

I sure hope my new father likes me. I saw a family picture. He's holding my baby sister. She looks kind of mean in her eyes, and she's holding a fist next to her cheek. But I hope she's sweet like Darlene is to Patrick. If I don't like her, I'll play with the cat and the dog. I'll call them Carla and Titti.

Can I tell you what I learned from people on this voyage? By the way, everybody is happy and friendly! (Well, I think Mr. Murphy will be happy, too, if he reads Patrick's comic books.) I learned that strangers can become friends. Before, I always wanted to be next to my Nonnis, but not anymore. I like playing, talking, and dancing with other people, too. I also learned that even though you miss your friends terribly, you can make new ones. Darlene says that if I join something called Girl Scouts, I'll have a whole group of friends.

Darlene told me that one day I'm going to have "crushes" on boys—just like her and Daniel. But can I tell you my first secret? There was a sailor in Genoa. He looked at me, smiled real big, and said to Nonna, "What a pretty girl!" I think I already have a crush on him. Maybe he's on this ship. I hope he kisses me like Daniel kisses Darlene.

I also learned something amazing. The world is so big! I used to think every place was small, like Pranzalito. But golly, this ship is a lot bigger than that! America is going to be huge! The first thing I'll see is the Statue of Liberty. She's in the ocean by New York. Nonna said she winks at immigrants. Nonno told me Detroit is a big city. I'll be riding lots of cars and going to baseball games and riding a bike on a paved street.

Well, enough for what I've learned. (You're probably get-ting tired of listening.) I'm excited that we'll reach America in two days! I think my mother is going to love the beautiful gold jewelry and Italian sweaters I brought for her. I can't wait to show her my First Communion dress! I know she'll love it.

I used to be scared of America—but not anymore. Darlene told me so much about it. I'll just do all the things she does: fashion shows, beehive hairdos, and the jitterbug. Her brother Patrick gave me some ideas on how to be more brave.

I'd like to ask you something. How can I get my Nonna to stop worrying about water? Can you write back to me, I wonder?

Arrivederci!

Piera

P.S. Can you help me meet movie stars in America?

Super Safety

— Tuesday, July 24 —

First Class

The Winter Garden lounge was where Daniel, his father, and Mr. Campi met. Mr. Campi, the *New York Times* journalist, had chosen the beautiful space on the ship for its quietness and its art.

"What do you think about this place?" Mr. Campi asked. "I like the primitive hunt scenes and thought it would inspire us to tell mankind what they have to do to survive. Your super ship will do just that, Daniel!"

"Sure, this is great," the young man replied with a slight lack of confidence. Art was not a field that interested him. Besides, he didn't have the answers that Mr. Campi hoped for.

"Victoria and I are fond of the Gambone panels," Richard Yates replied, referring to the giant ceramic wall panels by the renowned ceramic artist Guido Gambone. "We met the artist in London."

The journalist, anxious to end the small talk, pulled out his notebook in preparation for his own "hunt."

"So, Daniel, what can you tell me about your proposed super ship?"

Daniel squirmed in his chair. "Well, after what Dad told us, you know, that there is no such thing as an unsinkable ship and that—"

Daniel's father interrupted. "Daniel has decided that his internship paper would recommend new safety features on ships instead."

"You mean the *Doria* has room for improvement?" Mr. Campi asked with a skeptical smile. "Fine. Let's start with the lifeboats, since I know you studied them in detail. What did you think about them?"

Daniel looked at his father.

"Go ahead, son," Mr. Yates said.

"Well, they're sure better than the *Titanic's* wooden boats. They can carry more people and move faster and more safely because they're aluminum. They also have a built-in buoyancy feature." The reporter wrote quickly as Daniel continued. "They hold spare life vests and have food and other supplies. Some are motor propelled."

"But Daniel doesn't much care for the idea of lifeboats in general," Mr. Yates added.

Mr. Campi looked surprised. "Are you saying we don't need them onboard?" he asked, baffled.

"No, no. Not at all," Daniel replied. "But they have limitations. What if the ship suffered an incline of more than fifteen degrees, which is now the point when evacuation is suggested? The lifeboats would be extending out from the ship. How could they be boarded? And besides, on the opposite side of the ship, the davits would be facing the sky instead of downward. They wouldn't release to let the lifeboats descend."

Daniel's father was rather stunned at his son's smart conclusions. The journalist seemed equally impressed.

"What do you suggest instead of lifeboats?" Mr. Campi asked.

"A slide," Daniel answered. "It would shoot people quickly from the ship in case of fire or a steep incline from an accident."

"How would you store a long, heavy slide and get it over the railing?"

"It would be inflatable. And there would be inflatable tubs already on the water. People would slide down and drop into the tubs. There would be a cover that pops out in bad weather . . ."

Mr. Yates realized that the journalist needed time to write. He added, "Daniel studied the tragedy of the *Morro Castle,* a cruise ship that caught fire in 1930. One hundred thirty-seven people died from burns or from jumping into the water with their vests worn improperly."

"They broke their necks," Daniel said. "A shooter slide would eliminate injuries and could extend out far beyond a burning ship."

"Sounds like a good idea, Daniel," Mr. Campi said in awe. "Why hasn't anyone thought of that?"

Daniel shrugged timidly.

"Young man, I have a feeling you're going to be an inventor *and* a marine scientist. I'm going to be following your career. Whenever you come up with something new, let me know. I'll continue to report on issues of safety at sea with your suggestions."

The young scientist and his father beamed. Mr. Yates gripped Daniel's shoulder in a man-to-man gesture of pride.

At this point, the Campi, Yates, and Gibson girls walked in.

"Are you men talking ship stuff again?" asked eight-year-old Julie Campi. "Oh, I think I'm getting seasick." She pretended to fall dramatically. Everyone laughed.

"Can we go visit the dogs again, Daddy?" Lisa asked. "After yesterday's craziness, the crew put them back in the kennel."

"Sure. But make sure you all stay together."

The excited girls raced out just as Mr. Gibson showed up.

"Do you mind if I listen in?" he asked.

"Please do. Daniel is proposing safer ways to evacuate ships," Mr. Campi said.

"I'm very interested. I love my yacht, but you never know," the banker quipped.

"If you don't mind hearing about a futuristic idea . . ." Daniel waited for a response.

"Please, please," the three adults said.

"Here is my design for escape from ships and oil rigs." Daniel handed Mr. Campi his sketch. The journalist looked at Daniel, asking for clarifications about a design unlike anything he had ever seen. "Are these submarines or torpedoes?" he wondered.

"I know, I know. You think it's weird, but it's really the best way to evacuate a ship or a burning oil rig safely. These are like small submarines. They have a torpedo-like shape for steep entry into the water. They can travel underwater for quite a distance before bobbing back up. I deliberately designed them so if there's a lot of burning fuel around the ship, they have a pretty good chance of staying submerged until they're out beyond the flames."

"Brilliant. Absolutely brilliant!" Mr. Campi declared as he clapped quietly. "I admire your innovative spirit. We need people like you."

Mr. Gibson, showing his own approval and wishing to add his thoughts, said, "Meanwhile, let's hope you can build safer ships so evacuation doesn't come up again as it did with the *Titanic*. And if there should be an accident, let's hope we can count on our fellow man in life-threatening situations."

Something Awful

— **Wednesday, July 25** —

Piera

Dear Diary,

My Nonnis and I came in from a stroll because we couldn't see—the fog was so thick! And it made the decks so slippery that Nonna was afraid to slide off into the ocean. Even Nonno said the ship's foghorn needed to be "put out of its misery" because it sounded like a "wounded animal."

It doesn't matter. I'm so excited about the next two days. They might be the best days of my life! But I might not get to talk with you until I arrive in Detroit. Tomorrow we land in New York Harbor. I can hardly wait to see if the Statue of Liberty winks at me, like Nonna says she does. Then we fly to Detroit.

I'm really scared of going up in the sky in an airplane. It seems like a bad idea to leave the ground. What if the airplane engines stop working? I hope I never have to find out. As long as I get to meet my mother, my baby sister, and my new father, I'll be happy. I collected gifts for them on this beautiful ship: menus, daily programs, and a key chain that Nonno won at Bingo.

America is going to be so exciting! I can't wait to watch TV in the house and ride in a Rambler car. Everybody in Pranzalito says we're going to be rich in the New World. I hope they don't get jealous.

Don't worry, Diary. I'll keep you safe through all the moving around that's about to take place.

Your best friend,

Piera

P.S. Do you know how Titti and Carla are doing? I hope Aunt Lina doesn't forget to feed them.

Nonna said we were going to bid *arrivederci* to our shipboard friends tonight. *I wish we didn't have to. I don't want to leave this ship and their company. They're my friends now!*

"We'll go to the Social Hall on the Upper Deck, Piera. I know everyone's going to be there. But first, let's go visit Mr. Murphy in the hospital."

"How will he get off the ship if he can't walk, Nonna?" I asked.

"They'll carry him on a stretcher, Cici."

I'll tell her that in America I don't want to be called that anymore. I'm a big girl now.

Nonno wasn't thrilled about the idea of going to the Social Hall. "After dinner, I'm going to return to the cabin and begin resting for tomorrow's landing. Besides, I have to put our suitcases in the hall for the stewards. They're going to pick them up and place them on the starboard deck for unloading in New York."

We entered the hospital as Dr. Tortori was inspecting the big cast around Mr. Murphy's ankle. The patient welcomed our visit with the biggest smile yet. I didn't think it would be this sad bidding good-bye to a man who couldn't even talk to us. Yet Mr. Murphy had pulled at our heartstrings. It wasn't because he stuttered and was always frightened; it was something deeper. He seemed to be a broken soul who wanted to be unbroken. And seeing him go from being so shy to being "one of us" was awfully nice. He had even managed to make friends with the boy who hated boring adults! I planted a kiss on his cheek and waved *arrivederci.*

"Gggg- . . . dddd- . . . bbbb- . . . bye," he mumbled, wiping one eye.

As we turned to leave, I noticed two *Dennis the Menace* comic books on the dresser. *Patrick gave him another special gift,* I noted. Next to the comics was the mysterious tattered envelope that had passed from patient to doctor and seemingly back to the patient.

Later, we ate our final supper onboard.

Mrs. Henderson announced that there was going to be a band in the Social Hall afterward. "I hope they know how to play!" she said. "It's made up of passengers." People at several tables around us laughed.

"I invited Ruth Roman to come dance with us," Mrs. Marino joked, referring to the famous actress who was onboard. *Maybe she will show up.*

As usual, Patrick ran off before all of us, bumping into our chairs like a whirlwind tornado. His mother recited her daily chant, "I hope I can get that boy back to his father safe and sound," holding her hands in prayer and looking upward. "He's been nothing but trouble, that Dennis the Menace of mine!"

We appreciated her anxiety. And we were probably all wondering what he had up his sleeve for a "grand finale" that night—after all, his "grounding" was over.

❧

Chatter and cheery laughter filled the Social Hall.

All of our friends gathered in the bar area. Families hugged other families with teary eyes. Nonna was smiling—even laughing—as I hadn't seen her do for nine days. She must have felt so grateful at the thought of touching land again.

"It's been so nice watching Piera grow up on the voyage," kindly Mrs. Henderson said.

Nonna beamed and squeezed the cheeks of the three Henderson children.

Darlene gave me a big hug. I wanted to cry, but I knew she wanted me to be a big girl about this bittersweet moment.

"Let me see you smile, Piera," she said when she noticed my quivering lips. "We'll be writing often. I want to hear all about your new American wardrobe, OK?" She kept looking around, as if she was trying to spot someone. *Maybe Daniel's going to come say good-bye. She'll be sad not seeing him anymore . . . but maybe they'll get married one day.*

I spotted Patrick. He was watching band leader Dino d'Alessandra set up instruments in one corner.

Father Kennedy and Father Gardner, along with the three nuns, made their rounds. I heard them say "God bless you" over and over. Sister Angelica came to kiss me and said, "Welcome to the New World, Piera. You're going to like it." Then she added with a smile, "Don't forget to go to church!"

The athletic swimmer, Laura Dunes, explained that she had left Mariana with a babysitter in their cabin. She told everyone that she was dying to be reunited with her husband after being away all summer. "Mariana keeps asking, 'Where's Daddy?'"

Mr. Holmes rocked the baby twins in their buggy as Mrs. Holmes wished us well.

Nonna even welcomed them to America as if it was already her country. "We'll all have a big adjustment," she said, "but we immigrants are strong—maybe even stronger than Americans themselves." I felt so proud of Nonna. She had made this long journey in spite of her fear of water. And now she was preparing her mind for a new land.

The band began to play *"Arrivederci Roma,"* a song saying "so long" to Rome. Everyone whirled to the sweet strains on the dance floor. Nonna and I took a shot at the jitterbug.

At 11:00, Patrick stood in front of the band as if studying his next move.

Mrs. Dunes headed for the doors in a big hurry, briskly waving good-bye.

Someone asked her, "Why do you have to leave? Mariana's with a babysitter."

She kept running and mumbled, "I have to go . . ."

I hope Patrick comes over soon. I want to tell him I liked everything he did onboard and that he's really brave. He taught me to be ready . . . What is that noise???

All of a sudden, we felt a huge jolt. The bottles lining the bar all fell to the floor at once, with a scary crashing noise. Dancers froze like ice statues. The ship rocked over to the port side in a jerking swoop. Chairs, tables, and people flew through the air. Nonna and I tumbled to the floor. Then, as the vessel rolled back to the starboard side, we rolled along with it. Everything piled on top of us—sofas, chairs, tables, the band instruments—creating a cacophony of creepy sounds.

After a few moments of complete turmoil, we sat dazed, unable to speak. Then reality struck. Something truly awful had happened!

Should I cry? Nonna is safe, and she's not crying. Squeeze my hand hard, Nonna! No, hold me tight . . .

I began to cry for the first time on this journey.

Wails of despair echoed in the air. "Oh, *Dio!*" We heard God's name called out everywhere. Nonna made the sign of the cross over and over as her lips quavered in prayer. People tried to move about in search of their loved ones. They slipped and slid around, yelling, "*Papà!*" "*Mamma!*" "Stefano!" "Benedetta!" "Lucrezio!"

Nonna and I sat paralyzed with fear. *Where's Nonno? I wish he was here!*

Lights flickered on and off. Strange noises vibrated through the air: crashing and crumbling walls, scraping and crunching steel, screeching engines. *Where's all that noise coming from? Could it be the devil playing a cruel joke on us?* I recalled the nuns in Pranzalito saying that these things happened when humans least expected them.

People screamed, "*Titanic!*" over and over. *What does that mean?* I became more and more frightened as the "floating city" kept leaning more and more.

Suddenly, some people began taking running leaps up the big incline to the exit doors. *Where are they going? Where is there to go?* Nonna and I watched as many of them crashed back down. Those who made it onto the deck called back to report a frightful sight. "A big white ship inside us," a man announced, describing another vessel sticking through our hull. It had tried to pull out but was shaking so hard that it was rocking our even larger ship. Some described the sky as being filled with "fireworks," as white and orange sparks danced around a curtain of fog.

Inside the Social Hall, people tried to explain our dilemma. "We hit a mine from the war." "We hit an iceberg." "A boiler exploded."

Oh, no, we need Nonno to help save us! Why couldn't we stay in Pranzalito? Fear was now my big, bullying monster.

After some horrible moments, and to my great relief, I spotted Nonno coming through the Social Hall door. I first noticed his piercing blue eyes glassed over in fear; they looked bigger than I had ever seen them. *He's scared, too!* His hat sat crooked on his head as he clutched his briefcase to his chest. He was barefoot, and his pants legs were rolled up to his knees. He slid down the incline into our arms. *Thank God we're together!*

"Pedrin, what happened? What's happening to us?" Nonna begged my grandfather to explain.

He was breathless, both from the stress and from the awful climb up several flights of stairs. "I don't know. I heard a loud crashing sound . . . woke up, got dressed, and ran into the corridor. Water was gushing through. I smelled smoke and . . . hard to see . . . couldn't find the stairs . . . jammed . . . people screaming. They tried to pass me up onto the deck . . . complete chaos!"

"Oh, *Cristo!*" Nonna exclaimed as she squeezed me harder. "Why isn't anyone helping us? We could die!" This was the last thing I heard Nonna say for the following unbearable hours.

My grandfather put his briefcase in Nonna's lap and joined other men pushing heavy furniture from the low side to the high side of the list. *He's so brave, trying to balance our ship. Please, God, let this work!*

"Don't be fools!" a woman yelled in resigned desperation.

It was useless. The heavy objects all crashed back down, making people yell and swear at having to suffer more pain. Many were already bleeding from awful slashes and complaining of sprained or broken limbs.

Suddenly, we were startled by a long blast of the ship's horn, followed by several short blasts.

"Listen, the loudspeaker!" Nonno said. We strained but could not hear well, as people were still screaming hysterically.

"*Calmi . . . salvagenti . . . punti di riunione.*" We heard enough to know that we were in great danger. An officer was asking us to remain calm, get our life vests, and report to the muster stations.

But we don't have any life vests! I can't swim. Am I going to die? Where's Nonno going?

At random intervals, our luxury liner interrupted our continuous moans with muffled explosions, as it sank closer to the bottom of the sea. "We're going under! We're all going to drown!" a man hollered as he wobbled along the railing.

What is drowning? I wondered. It was a new English word for me.

Mrs. Henderson, huddled nearby with her three children, replied angrily, "Shut up! You're frightening my children!"

The man began to sob uncontrollably.

Perhaps he was right, but courage was the best weapon we had. It was difficult to ignore the brutal evidence all around us, however: the list worsening, horrific sounds amplifying, and revolting smells engulfing us. My Nonnis and I coughed as we inhaled smoke clouds of an ugly yellowish white.

How will anyone find us with fog outside and smoke inside? Are we going to die here? Now?

There was nothing left to do but recite familiar prayers. Many of us sat in prayer circles, hanging on to something for security—besides a rosary. Woeful wailing blended with "Hail Marys." The "now and at the hour of our death" part had taken on a new meaning. It made me shudder. And the quietness of praying made the creepy sounds from the vessel's bleeding bowels seem louder. The *Andrea Doria* was like a defeated prizefighter being socked continually in the middle and caving in each time.

I recalled Patrick's description of the sea monster in *Moby-Dick*—the one that bit off the captain's leg. It was all too frightening.

I wonder if Darlene, Patrick, and their mother are OK. Thoughts of friends raced through my mind.

I watched the priests and nuns. They were the only ones who didn't seem afraid. Father Kennedy and Father Gardner looked exhausted from going down the flooded corridors to bring up a half-dozen life vests at a time. We were so thankful, not because we expected to live but because of their kindness. Unfortunately, there weren't enough for my Nonnis and me. Then Father Kennedy began crawling on his knees around those most in shock. "Would you like to receive final absolution?" he asked over and over. Some, who truly believed that this was the hour of their death, said yes. The priest heard their confessions and gave them the last rites.

Sister Angelica was crawling around in her cumbersome black habit, saying words and prayers of comfort, always ending in "God bless you."

Nonna rolled her crystal beads through her fingers as Nonno felt the security of his briefcase.

Time passed slowly, yet it could not stop death's deep and dark approach as it slithered across decks and dark cavities.

Collision!

— *Wednesday, July 25* —

First Class

Lisa Campi was looking forward to the evening. Captain Calamai had accepted her invitation to join them for dinner. She planned to ask him to sign her autograph book. It was filled with celebrity signatures. Cary Grant, Jimmy Stewart, and Gregory Peck were among them. Lisa's birth father was something of a celebrity himself, a well-known radio man in the United States.

The Campis had decided to enjoy a walk on the Promenade Deck, as they had done before dinner for the last eight days. But tonight Lisa felt sadness, probably because of the gray shroud of fog that enveloped the shiny teak deck on three sides.

"I feel like I'm in an envelope!" Lisa said to her younger sister, Julie. "We should be celebrating our last night, but this fog . . ."

"Let's go to dinner a little early," Mrs. Campi suggested.

At the First Class dining-room door, they were met by the maître d'. "I'm sorry to inform you that the captain sends his regrets. He must remain on the bridge because of unusually heavy fog. He cannot even spare another officer."

Lisa was disappointed. She and her family had been so looking forward to dining in a special area with the special guest. But as a seasoned traveler, she knew that fog could play games around Nantucket. She hoped it would move out and the captain would change his mind.

The Yateses had also arrived early, explaining that they still had some packing to do after dinner.

Mr. Campi, always the journalist looking for sensational stories, tried to break up the light melancholy that everyone was feeling by joking around. "Wouldn't it be fantastic if the *Andrea Doria* crashed in the fog? Just think of the exclusive story I'd have for the *Times*!"

Mrs. Campi noted the startled—if not frightened—looks on the girls' faces. "Don't worry, girls. The captain has everything under control."

Margaret, Lisa, and Julie smiled again and peeked into Lisa's autograph book.

Mrs. Yates remembered how the girls had decided to play a game of "star spotting," in which they would report back how many movie stars they had identified onboard.

"I saw Ruth Roman and her son, Dickie!" shrieked young Julie, referring to the woman known for at least twenty Hollywood box-office hits.

"Lisa and I saw Betsy Drake," Margaret offered. "Her husband, Cary Grant, is shooting a movie in Europe, so he couldn't join her."

"I'm just glad I got to interview the captain," Daniel said.

Mr. Campi asked, "Did you collect all the data you need for your internship paper?"

Daniel looked at his father and nodded, assuring everyone that he couldn't have possibly learned more than he had during the eight days on the magnificent *Andrea Doria*.

Mr. Yates raised a glass of spumante. "Here's to a fabulous trip for all of us—and to great memories we've shared. It's been a pleasure getting to know you," he said, looking at the Campis. "Here's to meeting again." The crystal chimed cheerily.

After this final shipboard supper, the Yateses headed for their staterooms to pack, while the Campis decided to try their luck at the "horse races" one more time. Mr. Campi had won one hundred dollars at the races and another forty-five dollars at Bingo. He was hoping that his lucky streak would continue.

On this fog-darkened night, Captain Calamai decided to walk out on the bridge wing's observation platform, which extended beyond the hull of his ship eighty feet above the water. On a clear day, the captain would have a full view of the horizon. Tonight, his six-foot frame was cloaked in a heavy, murky vapor.

The master was preparing to square off against a shapeless phantom with an undetermined strategy. Mariners called it fog, an enemy that destroyed more ships than storms, coral reefs, or icebergs. Although it was not unusual for the area around Nantucket to brew warm currents from the Gulf Stream with icy northern waters, it was not to be taken for granted, either.

The captain reinforced the bridge with three other masters as a defense against Mother Nature's mysterious blinding form. They were assigned different instruments: one of the two radars, a gyroscope, and the loran for determining distances.

Captain Calamai phoned the engine room and ordered, "Reduce the speed." Reinforcements arrived to stand by in case fast maneuvering was needed. A large ship requires many sets of muscles to twist cumbersome valve wheels. Even so, stopping or simply slowing a great ship starts with a sluggish response.

"Close the watertight doors," the captain ordered an officer, who quickly began pressing switches that activated the safety partitions. Massive steel doors slammed shut and locked the ship into twelve separate waterproof compartments at the bottom portion of the vessel.

To warn other ships of his fog-obscured presence, the captain ordered, "Sound the whistle." A bellowing foghorn added an ominous feel to the muddy air; it roared relentlessly every one hundred seconds.

This high-traffic area was known as "The Times Square of the Atlantic." Captain Calamai shivered as he recalled the foggy night in 1934 when the White Star liner *Olympic* crashed directly into a Coast Guard vessel, the Nantucket Lightship, cutting it in half. His officers had complete confidence that Captain Calamai would navigate them safely to New York Harbor. But now, the *Andrea Doria* was headed straight for the same Lightship. "Steer three degrees to port," the master ordered as a correction.

The vapor from an hour earlier was now opaque, enshrouding the bridge and any distance beyond a half-mile. The two radar screens would become "eyes" for this obscure passage.

At 10:45, Officer Franchini yelled out from the chartroom, "It's a ship! We can see a ship."

The men went to peer into the radar, which displayed a bright green sweep line on a circular screen. Each sweep showed the other ship's advancing location. Since it was seventeen miles away, there was no reason for alarm, but the ship was moving east toward the *Andrea Doria*.

"I think it's unusual for a ship to be coming eastbound in these waters," Officer Franchini told the captain.

"Yes, it is very unusual," Captain Calamai replied.

Eastbound ships were supposed to be in a lane many miles

south of westbound vessels, allowing for safe passing—port-to-port or left-to-left. The captain was still calm, yet he was on alert about this starboard-to-starboard passage. *We're well apart,* he said to himself. He returned several times to the radar screens to verify the oncoming ship's position for himself.

The eastbound ship was approaching quickly. The officers realized that this was a fast-moving ship *and* traveling in an unassigned lane.

Officer Giannini felt to make sure that his gold crucifix pendant was in place. He noticed that his palms were sweaty but told himself, *We are still a safe distance away. If the other vessel maintains its course, all will be fine.*

The oncoming ship was now three and a half miles away.

"How close will she pass?" the captain asked.

"About one mile to starboard," Giannini replied, nervous but still not alarmed.

The captain turned to the helmsman and gave an order. "Steer four degrees to port."

It was 11:00. With each passing moment, the officers strained to sight the oncoming ship visually. They knew that radar was still not as precise as their own eyes, but the dense fog was robbing them of this advantage.

"Why don't we hear her?" Giannini asked the captain. "Why doesn't she whistle?"

The captain was now silent, perhaps focusing on his intuition, as there was not much time to discuss details or even strategy. He recalled watching American movies where the Indian chief, on horseback, sat perfectly still, as if calling upon all of his senses to decide when to raise his arrow and signal attack. Was this to be his unwanted battle?

As Officer Giannini aimed his binoculars out into the eerie night, an unbelievable sight met him head-on: the mast lights of the silent approaching ship were now visible and showing the port-side red light instead of the expected green.

"She is turning! She is turning!" Giannini exclaimed with a blood-curdling cry. "She is showing the red light. She is coming toward us!"

"I see her," the captain said faintly, his stare fixed rigidly on the other ship racing toward him at full speed.

Incredibly and inexplicably, the other ship was seconds from striking the *Andrea Doria* at full speed. Captain Calamai knew that he had to act instantly. He knew that in extreme situations, he had a choice to turn in whatever way he deemed wise.

"Hard left!" he shouted, the loudest he'd ever shouted in his life, as he faced his helmsman.

Would his liner respond in time to clear the collision? he wondered, his heart pounding hard enough to feel the beats in his head.

For several seconds, the captain stood immobilized. Officer Franchini realized this but knew that they had to signal their immediate left turn. He asked, "The two whistles?"

The captain nodded.

"The engines?" Franchini was suggesting that they should be shut down to lessen the blow.

"No! Don't touch the engines! We need all the speed!" It was the captain's intention to outrace the vessel that was about to broadside his.

At 11:10, the stunned officers of the pristine Italian liner saw a raging foe rip through a curtain of fog on the night water of the Atlantic. The captain clenched his teeth, awaiting the inevitable: the ramming of the *Doria's* starboard side.

God, let my passengers be saved! he said in a brief, silent prayer.

The men on the bridge and the lookout in the crow's nest braced themselves, helpless to save their prized liner. They watched in complete horror as a surreal, unidentified bow punctured the *Doria's* double hull. Screeches, groans, and crashes echoed for miles on the Atlantic. Sputtering sparks sprang from the friction of the massive crash. The calm silence of the night was transformed into a cacophony accompanied by grotesque fireworks.

Ten minutes later, the captain was able to identify his offender as it noisily withdrew from the *Doria's* entrails and he could read the name, "*STOCKHOLM.*"

"Dear God!" Officer Franchini exclaimed as he saw the mass of twisted steel that looked like the jaws of a monster, once the bow of the *Stockholm*.

As for the *Andrea Doria*, it now listed heavily, moaning mournfully and almost immobile.

Captain Calamai grabbed the railing, to maintain his balance and to assess the damage below. The V-shaped bow of the *Stockholm* was carved out of the *Andrea Doria's* hull. A flood of ocean water and oily substances swelled like torrents into the gaping hole.

Shocked and enraged, the officer's only remaining question was: Will the *Andrea Doria* stay afloat?

Without a minute to waste, Captain Calamai assumed a role that could only play out in a ship master's worst nightmares: saving his passengers while keeping his ship afloat, all the while seeking assistance from other travelers on the Atlantic. A brief thought about the *Titanic's* master, Edward Smith, came to his mind. How must he have felt under similar circumstances?

In his cabin, Officer Magagnini, second in command to the captain, had been rudely awakened by the shrill of two whistles and a violent blow to his cabin. Realizing that it was not a dream, he jumped out of bed, grabbed his flashlight, and headed for the bridge, still wearing his pajamas. Breathless, he arrived in time to hear the captain sending out distress signals to radio operators around the world.

"What happened?" Magagnini asked Officer Giannini, who immediately pulled him toward the loran screen.

"We've been broadsided at high speed by another vessel, the *Stockholm* . . . ripped open several decks . . . oil spilling out . . . already listing eighteen degrees."

As they spoke, the forward motion of the *Andrea Doria* ceased. The entire structure rocked, completely unstable, as sounds of collapsing steel punctuated the vaporous night. The officers watched the other vessel's lights retreat. The flagship of the Italian line, crafted for safety and beauty, was in danger of capsizing.

Officer Magagnini was overcome with rage. He loved the Andrea Doria; he had even hoped to be promoted to its captain one day.

"Reading on inclinometer?" the captain asked Officer Franchini.

"Eighteen degrees . . . now nineteen." The words had ominous implications for lowering the lifeboats.

"Officer Magagnini, go lower the port-side lifeboats."

Magagnini headed down to the Boat Deck as fast as his legs could move, hoping it wasn't too late. Two officers followed him on the slippery decks covered with moisture and splattered oil.

"Release the winch brakes!" he shouted.

They were all horrified to see the eight unresponsive lifeboats. They heaved with their backs, hoping to activate the mechanisms that released the davits from where the lifeboats hung.

Nothing. After several futile attempts, the tired officers returned to the bridge.

"Captain, the port-side lifeboats won't lower," Officer Magagnini reported.

Captain Calamai turned his head from this ugly news and continued to give his orders. "Officer Badano, make an all-ship announcement. Tell passengers in Italian and in English to report to their muster stations with life vests and stay calm."

"Shall I issue an abandon-ship order, Captain?"

Captain Calamai, in this most trying moment of his career—perhaps of his life—stood inert while facing the sea he had always loved. He then replied in a stoic voice, "No. It will only cause hysteria. There are only enough lifeboats for half of those onboard." Another flash of the *Titanic* came to his mind's eye.

Officer Badano took it upon himself to give an order to the engine room: "We must balance the ship by all means possible!" He was assured that every effort was being made.

It was after midnight. The inclinometer now read twenty-three degrees. The starboard side was listing so much that moving about the ship became extremely dangerous and difficult. The captain ordered the laying of grab lines to allow the staff to move about more securely. He then assigned the officers on the bridge to carry out evacuation at various stations around the vessel.

"Officer Magagnini, launch the starboard lifeboats," the captain said.

Daniel, who had rushed with his father to the bridge after the first jolt of the collision, felt that he had to help. After all, he had studied the lifeboats and their mechanisms in detail.

"I'll go with him," he announced, and his father looked at him in surprise.

"Daniel, are you sure?" his father asked.

Daniel knew that his father didn't expect a reply. He left with the first officer on a purposeful mission—to save lives. Thoughts raced through his mind: *We'll launch the lifeboats, then I'll go check on Darlene, her mother, and her brother. Then I'll survey the* Doria's *damage and be able to offer ideas for a future design.*

Nothing could have prepared Daniel for what he was about to witness. As they descended to the Upper Deck, he saw the massive destruction of cabins 52, 54, 56, and 58. His mind froze. He momentarily released his shock to think, *Cabins 52 and 54! Are Mr. and Mrs. Campi alive? What about Julie and Lisa? Maybe the family was still at the horse races during the ramming!*

As they continued toward the Boat Deck, the starboard incline seemed to grow relentlessly, submerging the *Doria* closer to the ocean floor. With each degree of list, the entire structure shook, releasing moans, groans, and creaks. Daniel shuddered as he braced himself along railings, yet he kept going.

Finally, he and Officer Magagnini arrived at the Boat Deck, followed by officers they had met along the way.

"Launch lifeboats!" the first officer commanded. As the winches released the davits, the lifeboats moved down. But because of the ship's extreme listing, they moved some twenty feet from the deck edge.

What can be done? No passengers will be able to board the boats safely this way, Daniel thought in a panic.

"We'll have to drop them into the water!" Officer Magagnini declared, although he realized that people would have to make their way to the ocean.

We'll have to lower people ourselves, Daniel figured, still eager to help.

The lifeboats smacked the water with force. Those toward the center front rocked violently as they sat in front of the gigantic gaping hole where tons of water assaulted the *Doria's* bowels.

Oh, God! I hope the Stockholm *didn't tear open more than two watertight compartments!* Daniel thought in horror.

It was now one hour after the collision. Daniel saw that the heavy fog was beginning to dissipate. In fact, he could clearly see people plunging into the ocean in their haste to get into a lifeboat.

I must find Darlene and her family, Daniel thought. *People are panicking. I'll tell her we've got things under control.*

Desperate families congregated at the stern. Some wept, others prayed with rosaries in hand, and still others plunged in despair into the black, shark-infested waters below.

"Have you seen Darlene Marino?" Daniel asked the people looking to him for help. "I need to find Darlene. Has anyone . . . Please, can you tell me . . ." Each time, he was met with shrugs.

The captain had ordered Officer Giannini to help with the starboard evacuation, and Giannini was already at work. Daniel watched as he and Officer Magagnini began unwinding fire hoses, Jacob's ladders, and nautical ropes, and then they began removing the netting that was covering the Third Class swimming pool.

Daniel reacted immediately to this brilliant idea, helping to tug and drag the heavy net and launch it along the side of the hull. The three men wanted to cheer, but that didn't seem appropriate. As people realized that this was their invitation to escape, they awoke from a shocked, inert state and mustered their courage to approach the dangling ropes and net. Daniel, several officers, medical personnel, and stewards began assisting passengers over the railing, where they crawled down the ropes and the net to the lifeboats crashing against the hull below. Some screamed with sheer fright, while others felt the pain of ropes burning their hands and bare feet. Others froze midway down and were told, "You'd better keep going, or I'll step on your hands!"

Daniel noticed the lack of panic, for the most part, and the fact that, amazingly, no fires had erupted on the ship.

Between 1:30 and 3:30 in the morning, the list had reached thirty degrees and was steadily worsening. With every wave entering the starboard side of the ship, it appeared that the stress of remaining afloat was becoming unbearable for the Grand Lady of Italy.

The slow evacuation continued. Some passengers became rescuers. A twenty-three-year-old man from First Class carried many screaming and biting children while swinging from a rope headed for the lifeboats. The captain had ordered children, the elderly, and women to be taken care of first.

"Daniel! Daniel!" someone yelled from below. Daniel looked over the railing, down to the ocean. Darlene had spotted him from her lifeboat. She was standing and waving. "We're here. We made it!"

Daniel released hours of anxiety by letting his body go limp and sink to the deck. He waved and yelled back, "Darlene! See you in New York!"

Daniel's curiosity was gnawing at him. He asked Officer Magagnini if they could check the conditions on B Deck before ascending to the bridge. They headed toward the bow. Along the way, they would pass in front of the garage. *I hope the Norseman was spared,* Daniel thought. The garage door was on the floor. The automobiles lay mangled, some flattened by collapsed steel bulkheads.

There's no use. It's over for these beauties.

It was nearly 4:00. The starboard list had reached more than thirty-five degrees.

Exhausted, Daniel and Officer Magagnini headed back to the bridge. The path reminded Daniel of a tornado zone he had seen in New England. The corridors were filled with rubble and collapsed cabins, wood, steel beams, girders, and furniture. Water gushed freely from many directions, including burst bathroom plumbing. Smoke seethed from burning electrical wiring. Everything—from every class—was obliterated, except for the chapel. As if God had decided, the sacred space had been spared.

How could this happen to the Andrea Doria? *It was supposed to be the safest ship . . . the most beautiful!* In his torment, Daniel felt driven never to let this happen again.

As they continued up and forward, Daniel saw the engine-room crew struggling to make their way to the bridge.

One engineer grabbed his head in his hands and said, "We had to abandon the engine room! One by one . . . areas flooded . . . the boilers and the diesel-dynamo space . . . generators stopped one by one. The fuel tank and deep ballast tanks ruptured, splashed hot flammable oil. We set the emergency pump in motion. The pump wouldn't work . . . too heavy a list. We took pails of oil from the engine room, carried them along the service passageway, leaning our backs against the bulkhead. Thank God, the emergency engine started! Then . . . no more electrical energy . . . we had to abandon . . ." The engineer and his crew looked spent and exasperated as they relived their agony.

Daniel could picture the large, noisy engine room as the engineer spoke. He had felt intimidated even under normal circumstances. How could they have worked down below when the ship was one-third flooded? He felt respect and sympathy for their physical and emotional pain.

"What about the watertight compartments?" Daniel asked.

"The bulkhead in between the two compartments was demolished," a crewman replied, shaking his head.

Daniel's spirits crumpled.

Exhausted, the men reached the bridge. Daniel turned his attention to the captain. *Dear Lord! He's aged ten years! He is the Ancient Mariner,* Daniel thought, reminded of the famous poem.

Daniel overheard the captain say something disturbing to Officer Badano, who looked troubled.

"If you are saved," Captain Calamai said, "go to Genoa, and tell my daughters I did my duty."

What does he mean, 'If you are saved'? Does he mean he would . . . Dear God . . ."

Officer Badano placed his hand on the captain's shoulder and emphatically said, "Captain, we will *all* be saved!"

Daniel looked around for his father. "Where's my dad?" he asked.

Officer Badano said he had heard from him on the wireless

radio. Mr. Yates and Officer Giannini had gone to find passengers stranded on the high port side. They had no way of knowing that lifeboats had arrived. The two men and a nurse were escorting them to the starboard side. They tied ropes around passengers' life vests and lowered them to the ocean.

Mr. Yates and Officer Giannini soon returned. They were covered with black grease and a heavy layer of perspiration. The father and son gave each other a quick man-to-man embrace, and Mr. Yates said, "I saw that your mother and Margaret got a proper send-off to the rescue ship. I told them we loved them very much."

The young man reflected on this seemingly innocent comment. *Of course, we love them! Why is he saying that now? Does he think . . .?*

Rescue and a "Ride from Hell"

— *Thursday, July 26* —

Piera

"The rescue ships have arrived! They're sending us lifeboats. We must abandon ship now!"

Oh, Dio! I don't want to go into the water. And Nonna is going to be too scared.

The crewman urged us to crawl up the incline to the doors. "I'll guide you to the starboard side where the lifeboats are waiting."

Spirits lifted, and swollen limbs dragged their way out onto the deck. We made a human chain by hanging on to one another while pressing our backs to the railing. Some people fell and slid across the slippery deck, only to crash against the pool or the outer railing.

Hang on to me, Nonnis! I don't want to slide into the ocean!

We reached the low, listing starboard side. It was strewn with suitcases. The Marinos were standing in line to make their descent. Little Patrick, the ship menace, was telling them to jump! *Isn't he scared of the sea monsters?*

The four young German men who played Ping-Pong every day became our angels of mercy. "Here. I tie this rope around your waist," one said. "We lower you down there."

"No, *non posso!* I'm not going!" I protested with a scream.

Incredibly, my Nonnis encouraged me to leave their side— that warm umbilical strand that had served me for nine years. My new safety cord was now a thick rope tied around my waist. I cried to my lungs' full volume, and perhaps beyond, as I dangled above a swaying lifeboat far below.

"Be brave, Cici! We're coming down, too!" Nonna yelled down.

The descent lasted forever. Finally, a crewman guided my legs into the boat. "You're fine now, *chérie,*" he said with a French accent.

I want my Nonnis! Please come down! I feared separation from them more than anything.

I looked up and saw something most amazing. Nonna lifted her leg over the railing, grabbed the rope, and made her way down, all while her purse swung from her arm. I silently cheered her. But then I saw that she was headed for the black water. An image of a sea monster flashed before my eyes. *She's going to lose her leg!* I let out a shrill cry that seemed to alert a crewman, who grabbed Nonna's legs and pulled her into the lifeboat.

What about Nonno? I don't want to leave without him.

The lifeboat was crowded. Looking up to the Upper Deck, we could see Nonno gesturing with the Germans. They seemed hesitant. The Frenchman signaled them to send him down. Nonno grabbed the rope, twirled and twirled, his hat on his head, his briefcase in hand, until he landed hard in our lifeboat. We cried as we held one another. Some comfort at last!

But it wasn't over. We looked up and saw that it was Patrick's turn to descend. He had decided not to jump after all. He boldly grabbed the rope and forced it to make big swirls over our heads. *He's smiling, that daredevil! He thinks he's a circus act.* I briefly forgot my plight. Then everything changed. Pat's life vest got hooked on something, and he couldn't move. Everyone around us began screaming for the boy's life. "Somebody's got to help him!" a man near us shouted.

"Nonnis, that's Mr. Murphy running down the stairs!" I yelled out. Our once fearful friend had heard our pleas and jumped off the stretcher. Holding on to the railing with both hands, he took flight, even with his ankle cast! He reached his shipboard buddy, unhooked him, watched him grab the rope again, and climbed back up the stairs, dragging his right foot behind him. As Darlene and Mrs. Marino descended, Mr. Murphy continued to climb up and down stairwells, each time with a child in tow. Nonna made the sign of the cross every time.

Just as our lifeboat began rowing away, Darlene yelled, "Daniel! Daniel!" My friend had somehow spotted the young man lowering passengers along the Second Class stern.

He leaned over the railing, waved, and hollered back, "I'll see you in New York!"

By now, the fog had completely lifted. People said that God had swooped it away with his mighty arms.

Our lifeboat managed to escape the swells created by tons of water gushing into the big hole in the wounded liner. We also escaped the giant funnel tilting parallel to the water, shining an eerie red glow, like that of a witches' cauldron. We could not escape a ghoulish sight in the distance: the mangled steel that was once the strong ice-breaking bow of the *Stockholm*. It looked as if the jaws of a famished animal had been destroyed as it devoured its kill.

We began our "ride from hell." Crossing a mile of debris was as nauseating as the vomit that dirtied the lifeboat. Suitcases, wood beams, clothing, and even a baby buggy bobbed aimlessly around us. *I hope the twins are safe! I didn't think that crossing the ocean would be this awful. Poor Nonnis! They must be wishing they were back in Pranzalito.*

We rowed toward the rescue ship. It was like a mirage in the middle of the ocean. But its rows of twinkling lights unmistakably spelled out "*Ile de France.*"

Still traumatized, we found it hard to grasp this miracle. People were still lamenting ridiculous things: "I left my teeth in the bathroom." "My new suit is ruined." "How can I let my American family see me barefoot?" I admit that I wondered if I would ever see my First Communion dress again. But this was a time to feel grateful. There were certainly passengers left behind who wished they had lost only their possessions! *I hope no one died! Where are our friends?*

We finally pulled up alongside what looked like an ocean skyscraper. *Oh, no, I don't want to climb up that high ladder! I could fall into the ocean!* I wondered how we would get through the window at the very top. A man urged me onto the rope ladder and promised to stay behind me. How could I not look down at my feet? Flares from the rescue ships crisscrossed over the black sea to provide light. I pressed on to the top. A French seaman pulled me in with a kind "*bonsoir.*" It was going to be a good evening—finally! My Nonnis soon followed.

We collapsed into lounge chairs. Later, we indulged in the hospitality of the French luxury liner, serving croissants, soup, sandwiches, and coffee. They gave blankets to those who were scantily clad. Word got around that the ship had been headed to France but had turned back in the dangerous fog to come save us. We were thankful.

One by one, our shipboard friends arrived. We huddled in grateful misery. Everyone seemed anxious to share brave survival stories.

"I tied the buggy to the rope and lowered the twins," Mr. Holmes explained. "And Mr. Murphy brought the other children to the railing so a crewman could carry them down to the lifeboat."

Everyone gasped. *And I thought he was afraid! He got really brave!*

Mrs. Holmes reminded us of her premonition. "I was right! Remember how I imagined that the twins were floating on the sea in their cradle?" We smiled awkwardly.

Mrs. Dunes rocked agitatedly while clutching little Mariana as she spoke. Her face was covered with oil smears under her baseball cap. "We were on a dark deck. The lifeboats couldn't see us, so I had to do something. It was awful!" She began to sob as Mariana stroked her face. "I tied a rope around Mariana's waist and dangled her alongside the ship so the lifeboat would see her. Poor thing. She got scared, raised her arms, and yelled 'Mamma!' Her body slipped through the rope and fell into the water."

Mrs. Dunes was out of breath as she relived this horror. "I yelled, 'My baby is in the water!' but there was nobody to help. So I dove in. But I couldn't find Mariana below the surface. I went under again, and her little body rubbed against mine." The young mother sobbed as we all wiped our tears. "You know, I already knew ten minutes before the collision that Mariana needed me!"

I spotted Father Kennedy and Father Gardner praying with many families. They also stopped to console those who were alone. Sister Angelica walked about with a smile. "God bless you," she offered to those who appeared most in shock. A young couple with two toddlers begged her to look for their missing three-year-old daughter.

"We had to take different lifeboats. They took off with our other daughters, but we can't find Maria. Thank God we found our two youngest," they said, hugging their girls.

The most surprising story came from Mrs. Marino. Patrick sat next to her, subdued. "My son is a hero! Patrick and I were watching a movie in the dining room when the big boom threw us off our feet. I started crying, 'My baby, my baby!' Patrick said, 'Mom, I'm here.'" She began to smile. "I stupidly said, 'Not you! Darlene!' This boy ran out like lightning. Somehow he found his way to the cabin—thanks to all of his exploring—in all that smoke and water gushing in the halls. He found his sister fast asleep, and the bow of that monster—you know, the *Stockholm*—was one inch from cutting through her body!" Patrick nodded humbly. "He slapped her awake, then grabbed her and pulled her out of the cabin as it was filling with water!"

I'm glad she's proud of Patrick. She always thought he caused trouble.

Darlene, teary-eyed, hugged Patrick and said, "My brother's my hero!"

"Now we have to pray that Mr. Murphy got off the ship alive. He saved my son!" Mrs. Marino said.

High-pitched strains from a woman singing something from the opera *Aida* interrupted Mrs. Marino's incredible story. Wrapped in a blanket, the woman bellowed in a way that teetered on hysterics. Seeing that she was out of control, the ship doctor ran to inject her with a tranquilizer. She crumpled to the floor.

Mrs. Henderson and her three children had been listening intently to others' horrific stories. The mother said, smiling, "I forced my children to be brave. I pushed them off the deck into the water, one by one. They protested, but I had no choice. No one was around to help."

"How did you get to the lifeboat?" asked Mrs. Dunes, concerned about the other woman's pregnant condition.

"I crawled over the railing, jumped while holding my knees to my chin to protect my belly, and landed among my children. Randy's really mad at me for pushing him."

The ten-year-old, who had been pouting, turned his head away from his mother. His older brother, Pete, managed to find some humor among the drama: "An old man threw his suitcase overboard, and it almost hit us. Someone said, 'Look at that fool's suitcase. It's drowning!'"

Although each story was fascinating, I succumbed to my exhaustion and didn't wake up until we disembarked in New York.

My Nonno was able to send a telegram to my mother: "*Tutti salvi—arrivederci.*" All saved—we'll be seeing you.

Abandon Ship

— Thursday, July 26 —

Survivors

Daylight was breaking. A new sun was revealing the night's horrific destruction all around the *Andrea Doria*. From the bridge, the men passed around binoculars to examine the debris, making sure that no one was using it for flotation. Open suitcases, strips of wood, mounds of metal, and even life rings were evidence of a lost night and lost dreams.

And what about the loss of life? Surely the people whose cabins had been plundered by the *Stockholm's* bow had been washed out to sea. Were there any still alive onboard, trapped and suffering?

One by one, officers, stewards, the doctor and a nurse, and the chaplain returned to the bridge. Their beard-stubbled faces and black-blotched clothes indicated a long sleepless night. No one complained, though. They gave their reports.

"No one's left on Boat Deck."

"The stern on all levels is abandoned."

"First Class cabins empty."

"Third Class completely vacated."

Each survivor-rescuer, sitting or lying on the deck, looked at the captain for direction.

Captain Calamai used the emergency power still feeding the bridge to communicate by radio with the Coast Guard: "Request towing of my ship."

Mr. Yates knew that this was impossible. He looked at Daniel, shaking his head. Then he lay on the port-side deck and looked way down to the ocean. He discovered what he had suspected: the bilge keel, a balance fin usually deep under the vessel, was exposed. That meant that the ship was close to capsizing.

The naval architect wanted to explain this to the captain, but what was the use? The captain's mind was set on towing, his last attempt to rescue his grand lady and perhaps his reputation. Everyone sensed that the *Andrea Doria*, still inhaling water, would be too heavy and too structurally weak for towing. And to where? If they were dragged to the shoals of Nantucket, how would rescue boats get to them in such shallow waters?

Officer Magagnini broke the icy silence of the warm, breezy morning. "Master, there is nothing left to do. We have inspected every part of the ship. The passengers have all been evacuated. We must abandon ship."

"You go. I'm staying," the captain replied sternly.

The officer assumed that the captain wanted to wait for the tow barge. He also appreciated the captain's reluctance to abandon his ship. The law of the sea would give ownership to whoever boarded an empty vessel.

Meanwhile, Officer Magagnini ordered the twenty remaining passengers into the lifeboats. Since the list was now forty degrees, they could almost walk off the deck into the three remaining vessels. One by one, they descended a ladder. Magagnini looked up, astonished to see his captain standing firm.

"Come down!" he hollered at him.

Captain Calamai signaled that he was remaining exactly where he was.

Magagnini and Officer Badano both realized that the captain would be willing to sacrifice himself for his ship.

"If you don't come down, we'll all come up!" the first officer threatened. His captain continued to stand firm. The officer began climbing the ladder, with his officers lined up behind him; they were ready to give their lives for their hero.

Realizing the danger in which he was placing his crew, Captain Calamai finally gave up. At 5:30 on the morning of July 26, the grand lady of the Italian line was left to fend for herself.

❧

Three tiny vessels bobbed on a vast ocean. Their destination: the American fruit freighter *Cape Ann,* which stood patiently in the distance. Just as the other rescue ships had done, it remained distant from the sinking *Andrea Doria.* They feared being sucked into a giant whirlpool if the Italian liner were to sink.

Daniel and his father, in the lifeboat following the captain's, were appalled at the size of the damaged hull. "It appears to be about sixty feet wide," Mr. Yates pointed out, "but look at the long tear. The *Stockholm's* bow ripped everything open like a can opener opening a sardine can!"

Feeling pity yet admiration, Daniel remarked, "It's surprising she hasn't sunk already. Remember what you said about not expecting more than a fifteen-foot penetration? It looks twice that size, and the two watertight compartments flooded. She's amazing! Dad, why does the big hole have such jagged edges?"

The naval architect shook his head in sorrow. "When the *Stockholm* put its engines in reverse, it probably shook terribly. It might have been wiser to remain implanted. By pulling out, it tore more of the hull and left that giant hole."

Daniel looked down and wondered, *Who was in those cabins? Could anyone still be alive?*

The lifeboat occupants saw the signs of desperate survival:

ropes, sheets, and nets strung along the hull; oil-slicked decks with marks from human hands groping and sliding across them. One question was uppermost in all their minds: *How could this have happened?*

Captain Calamai, sitting alone at the back of the lifeboat, still wearing his blue beret, uttered not a word. He was reflecting on eleven hours of horror. *Why did they turn into us? We did everything to turn away from them. Did someone misread his radar?*

The *Andrea Doria* master looked out at his beloved ship. It reminded him of an abandoned ghost town he had seen in an American film. There seemed to be no good reason. Even in the *Titanic* movie, they showed a solid reason. He rewound the projector in his mind to replay the bitter aftermath of the collision.

How many passengers are lost? How many injured? And the crew? Good thing the engine-room crew survived. Too bad the Coast Guard couldn't send planes and helicopters; the fog was so thick. At least the helicopters finally picked up the injured this morning.

So many rescue ships! So many brave sailors! I will thank them in New York. I'll thank the Stockholm, *too, for sending their lifeboats. A sailor's biggest glory is to participate in a rescue. A captain's worst defeat is to abandon his ship. But I had to! I hope I will be forgiven.*

I used to love the sea. Now I hate it! I'll never sail again!

The captain's silent soliloquy stirred in his mind like the *Doria's* propellers had stirred the waters.

❦

After a brief respite on the *Cape Ann,* the last of the survivors returned to their three lifeboats to board the U.S. Navy destroyer escort, the *Allen.*

When they climbed onboard, they faced a surprise. News reporters had come to interview the captain and the crew. Microphones were shoved in front of them. "Tell us what happened?" "Why didn't you turn before?" "Why didn't you slow down?" "Why . . .?"

Captain Calamai retreated to the *Allen's* office, but the *Andrea Doria* expert, Mr. Yates, faced the questions.

"Why did the accident happen?"

"We don't know. I'm sure there will be a full inquiry," Mr. Yates replied.

"Why didn't the captain order a right turn, as maritime law says to do?"

"This was an extreme situation. He was allowed to use his judgment. We could have killed everyone onboard the *Stockholm.* We tried to escape the blow to both ships."

"Why didn't the *Doria* reduce her speed in fog?"

"Fog is very dangerous, so there was some reduction in

speed, and our foghorns were blasting. The captain reinforced manpower on the bridge. All was according to maritime law."

Daniel was in awe of his father's command of the questioning. The interrogation seemed repetitious and endless, yet Mr. Yates patiently informed the media.

"Why didn't the captain issue an abandon-ship order?"

"There weren't enough lifeboat spaces. He was afraid that passengers would have fought one another for the spaces available."

"Why have passengers already filed a formal complaint against the captain and the crew for not helping them get rescued?"

Mr. Yates was shocked to hear this. He asked himself, *Can this be true? I was one of the rescuers. We helped everybody we could find off the ship.*

"I'm unaware of such a complaint," he replied.

"Is it true that many of the crew were cowards, that they abandoned the ship before the passengers?"

Daniel, infuriated by the unfairness of the questions, could no longer remain silent, although he had never spoken into a microphone before.

"I personally saw crews giving their vests to passengers. They helped evacuate others—the sick, the elderly, infants—by carrying them down the ropes, without wearing life vests! How could you . . .?"

Mr. Yates, realizing that his son might be too emotional to respond wisely, interrupted. "We have been working through the night. I'm sure you understand that we need to get some rest after being awake for nearly twenty-four hours."

The occupants of the last lifeboats, tasting bitter defeat, pushed through the huddled media. Their ordeal would not be over for a long time.

Safe Harbor

— *Thursday evening, July 26* —

Piera

By a miracle, the *Ile de France* brought us to the New World only twelve hours late. As we approached the harbor, crowds of people cheered and waved banners. Camera flashes popped. It all made us feel important—but at an unthinkable price!

"Where is the Statue of Liberty, Nonna?"

My grandmother hugged me and said that she had decided to let me sleep when we passed her. *I wish I could have waved to her!*

We were escorted into a huge, strange-looking building. "Piera, China, Pedrin!" we heard someone call out. I felt arms around me. It was my great-aunt, Teresa. She bent down, looked straight into my eyes, and asked worriedly, "Are you all right?" My Nonnis nodded for me and wept uncontrollably.

A handsome man was standing there. Aunt Teresa said,

"Piera, this is your father." We shook hands.

As we walked toward a buffet area, Nonna rambled, telling one story and then another, gathering pity as her arms made swoops in the air. "An awful noise . . . we went up in the air. People were hurt . . . some washed out to sea. We lost everything . . . everything gone . . . our beautiful ship!"

Nonno held his briefcase tightly; one latch was broken. "Don't we have to show our passports?" he asked.

My new father, Lino, shook his head and said, "No, not on this trip."

"Are you hungry, Piera?" Aunt Teresa asked.

"I want that," I said, pointing to some glass-like squares of orange, red, green, and yellow.

"That's Jell-O. But you need meat and fish. You've been up for forty hours."

"Please! I just want Jell-O." I was stubborn from sheer fatigue. I was curious to try my first American food. It wiggled in my mouth.

My aunt then suggested that we telephone my mother so she could hear my voice. Nonna coached me to tell her that she was beautiful. It was the only English word she knew. On the line, I heard a strange voice say, "Hello?" So I said, "You are beautiful." There was crying.

The loudspeaker announced the names of survivors. People sat in prayer, with anxious, dark-circled eyes.

Aunt Teresa said that our flight for Detroit would be leaving in a few hours. I was too tired to be scared of yet another adventure. Besides, soon I would see my mother. *I bet she's pretty.*

Flashbulbs and Microphones

— *Thursday evening, July 26* —

Survivors

People pressed tightly against one another, shoulder to shoulder, at New York Harbor. Thousands had gathered to await the arrival of the rescue ships carrying hundreds of *Andrea Doria* survivors. The crowd's mood was mixed: joy among those who knew that their loved ones were arriving, deep anxiety among those who knew nothing.

The *Ile de France* began to unload its passengers. *Andrea Doria* survivors walked across the footbridge first, all 753 of them. TV reporters stood on each side of the bridge, ready to grab details for a good story. "Are you hurt?" "Did you lose anyone?" "How did you get rescued?" Most survivors walked past hurriedly. Others peered into the cameras and offered personal reports.

"Please ask if anyone has seen Maria," asked a young father accompanying his family.

A reporter announced, "It's the mayor of Boston! Sir, please tell us about your experience."

The distinguished-looking man, standing next to his wife who had a black eye, shook his head. He said, "I don't know how we survived. I came out of the bathroom and found the cabin swirling with water. My wife was about to be swept away. I tugged on her with all my might and dragged her into the corridor." His wife bowed her head, hiding her deep emotions from public view.

The procession of haggard *Andrea Doria* passengers continued.

"Look, everyone, it's Hollywood actress Ruth Roman. She's got a big smile," the reporter announced. "Miss Roman, you appear unhurt."

"Yes, but my son Dickie is missing. He was taken by a different lifeboat." An anxious look replaced her wide grin.

The reporter prodded. "How did the crew treat you?"

"They were wonderful. One steward even warmed milk for the children. And we all discovered that we have an amazing inner resource—strength to pull us through against great odds."

"And finally, here is the captain, undoubtedly one of the heroes of this incredible rescue. Captain de Beaudéan, how do you feel about saving so many lives?"

"I did my duty," the captain of the *Ile de France* replied, beaming, with a heavy French accent. The crowd cheered wildly.

"Why did you decide to risk your passengers' lives by turning a huge ship in heavy fog?"

"A ship as large as the *Andrea Doria* would not send an SOS unless it was in trouble. I followed my instincts." The cheers moved up another notch.

A woman in pain from multiple injuries passed by on a stretcher, sobbing.

The reporter said, "Captain, can you tell me about this woman?"

"She's Josephine Campi. She told me she believes her family was killed. They were in the cabins directly hit by the *Stockholm's* bow—fifty-two and fifty-four, I think."

The reporter said, "Let's all pray for the family and hope that there is some good news for the woman."

The throngs now headed off in search of loved ones or simply more information.

"Ladies and gentlemen," a reporter announced, "we just got news that the naval escort ship *Allen* has arrived. The Italian captain and his crew are supposedly onboard. This should be quite a story."

Chaplain Natta, Dr. Tortori and his nurse Antonia, and several crew members and stewards walked solemnly across the bridge. Mr. Richard Yates and his son were among them.

"Tell us, what did you learn from the horrible accident? Didn't your company insure the *Andrea Doria?*" the TV reporter asked Mr. Yates.

"Yes, and rightly so. She lived up to the finest maritime standards."

"So why did she sink? Wasn't she supposed to be unsinkable?"

Daniel, disturbed by the question, spoke authoritatively into the microphone. "No ship is unsinkable. And no ship has been built to withstand such a terrible impact. But now we know that marine scientists need to devise more safeguards. I plan to—"

Daniel's explanation was abruptly interrupted.

"And here is Captain Calamai himself! Captain, how do you feel about losing your ship?"

Captain Calamai, still wearing his blue beret, stood stunned at the thoughtless question. He looked worn and defeated. Two U.S. Navy officers in white stood at his side, each holding one of his arms.

The TV reporters continued: "Captain, there's been a lot of rumors. Did you or did you not give an abandon-ship order?"

Captain Calamai maintained his silence as the reporters kept grilling him. "How did the accident happen?" "Did the radar malfunction?" "Did the crew abandon ship?" "Where were you . . .?"

The captain of Italy's maritime jewel did what he felt was best—he exited the scene.

The crowd was silent.

Flashbulbs popped, reporters scrambled, and the throngs began to make their way toward another pier. The wounded *Stockholm* was pulling into the slip it had left only the day before.

A TV announcer planted at the edge of the bridge began: "There is a lot of excitement as we await the debarkation of more *Andrea Doria* survivors arriving on the *Stockholm*. And Captain Nordenson is one of the heroes for saving more than five hundred lives."

Looking out at the ocean, the reporter exclaimed, "Oh, how awful! The bow . . . it's all mangled, and a lot is missing! It seems to be holding on to wood boards, steel beams, and . . . How did that ship stay afloat?"

Another announcer interrupted. "Nik, while you're waiting for the *Stockholm's* debarkation, we have a news flash. Popular songwriter Mike Stoller, who was on the *Andrea Doria*, has debarked from another ship. His music partner, Jerry Leiber, is here to welcome him. Let's hear what they have to say."

"Oh, man, you're OK! Hey, Mike, we've got a smash hit!" Jerry declared.

"No kidding?" Mike said.

"I'm not kidding. 'Hound Dog.'"

"Big Mama Thornton?" Mike asked, referring to the blues artist who had originally recorded the tune.

"No, some white kid named Elvis Presley."

"And now let's get back to our coverage, Susan. I hope you have more good news from the *Stockholm*," the announcer said.

"Well, right now, it's not looking so good," said the reporter. "There's a line of stretchers. The Red Cross is running toward them. This is awful! A teenage girl. Does anyone know who she is?"

A small Latin-looking man replied, "I do. Everyone's calling her the miracle girl. I found her on the tip of the smashed bow, on her mattress! She was bloody. I asked her name. She said she was Lisa Campi. We looked up her name on the ship's manifest but couldn't find it. We realized she had been on the *Doria.*"

The reporter looked shocked. "Well, then, how did she get onto the *Stockholm's* bow?"

"We believe the bow hit her cabin, number fifty-two, and when the bow pulled out, the girl was lifted off her bed."

"How can she be alive? This is truly a miracle!"

The Red Cross nurses rushed to follow the stretcher to a black limousine. They injected the "miracle girl" with pain medication.

The reporter continued. "And who is this man on crutches? He's got a heavy cast around his ankle. Sir, please, tell us your name."

"Ernest Murphy," he replied. His roommate stood by his side.

"Wait, that name sounds familiar. Oh, yes, the renowned philanthropist."

Mr. Murphy's roommate interjected, "And now, a renowned rescuer. This man," he said, laying a hand on his shoulder, "is responsible for saving many, many children."

"How did you do that while wearing a cast, sir?"

"I was grateful for the opportunity," Mr. Murphy replied with a wide, confident smile. As he walked away, he pulled an oil-stained envelope out of his torn pocket and threw it into the air, as if in celebration.

The reporter fumbled to grab it before it reached the ground. He opened it and read, "'Dear Dr. Tortori: This man may need sedation when traveling on the *Andrea Doria*. He has a dreadful fear of ocean travel. Moreover, he is plagued by nightmares describing a frigid scene in a lifeboat. He often yells out, 'How can we just leave them?' It is my assumption that, as a survivor of the *Titanic*, a sense of survivor's guilt has led to his stammering handicap.'"

The reporter added, "It's signed by psychologist Dr. Raoul Wiseman. A *Titanic* survivor? That's incredible! But wait, did the doctor mention stammering? I don't recall any stammering."

After pausing, the reporter concluded, "Ladies and gentlemen, I think we have witnessed the miracle of self-forgiveness, the blessings of redemption."

The reporter signed off, saying, "This is Nik Worthy, standing among the brilliant characters of the greatest sea rescue in peacetime history. Good night."

Epilogue

Pierette

Thanks to our brave rescuers, all but forty-six *Andrea Doria* passengers and five *Stockholm* passengers reached New York. The Red Cross and others helped those in need of medical and other assistance. Maria Sole Pilla was reunited with her parents after having spent two days at the New York City shelter. Many needed help in planning transportation to their final destinations. It must have been frightening to travel at all, much less alone in this new land.

As for me, it was a bittersweet arrival in Detroit. At the airport, it felt strange to be surrounded by two families, one old and one new. I gave my mother—who was really a stranger to me—the biggest hug I knew how to give. Her tears and her worried look told me that she had agonized over our ordeal. She said later that for many hours, she did not know if we were alive. The raving beauty I had seen in photographs was a pretty woman, mostly in a maternal way. I admired her sense of fashion. I was disappointed that I couldn't find a family resemblance.

The small bungalow we now would call home was much smaller than our farmhouse in Pranzalito. It had to accommodate five of us, including a baby who cried incessantly from colic.

We did indeed have a TV, but the first things we watched were replays of the *Andrea Doria* sinking. We cried endless tears for having lost all of our beautiful family heirlooms—and realizing that we could have joined them at the bottom of the sea. We prayed for those who perished. Reports about the Campis were grim. Only Lisa, the "miracle girl," and her mother had been found.

Remarkably, deep-sea divers had reached our sunken liner—and even recovered a suitcase. I felt broken-hearted that it wasn't ours. As for the Ascoli jewels, the sea must have claimed them, along with their heiress.

The saddest thing of all was how reporters hounded Captain Calamai. "*Il povero uomo,* the poor man," my Nonnis would say. They felt sorry for him. He was being held responsible for the collision and the sinking of his liner. He was also criticized for how he carried out the rescue, although he had led the most successful maritime rescue in peacetime. All the while, the captains of the rescue ships, including Nordenson of the *Stockholm,* were being congratulated.

Captain Calamai was never asked to command another ship.

He died in 1972. His last words were "Are the passengers safe?" Those who knew him said that he died of a broken heart.

My life took on some normalcy. Every day was a new adventure: going to school, joining Girl Scouts, studying ballet and the violin. It took six months for me to learn English fluently; everyone was proud.

My grandparents struggled to communicate outside the home. Nonna continued to be afraid of water. I became an excellent swimmer.

We lost contact with our shipboard friends, but we did read about many of them throughout the years. Some achieved a great deal of success. A few wrote about how the *Andrea Doria* tragedy had ruined their lives.

My Nonnis refused to discuss the *Andrea Doria;* it was too painful. We did read some articles, including one that made us laugh. Patrick Marino had become a media darling after people heard of his escapades. One article said that to escape questioning, the youngster took cover by climbing a tree. He did tell the press that he remembered one thing: looking at his shiny new bike sitting on deck just before he grabbed the rope to the lifeboat. Reporters would ask, "Do you remember the accident?" And he would reply, "I don't care if that ship sank! I just want my racing bike and my thirteen *Dennis the Menace* comic books!"

Patrick continued to believe that his friend had cast a jinx on the *Andrea Doria.* "I beat him up, and he said, 'I hope your ship sinks.'"

I'm not sure why we were destined to be on the last voyage of the *Andrea Doria*. What I do know is that the experience has given me strength to make my life journey with grace.

The blessing of immigration is that two cultures have enriched my life. Yet I don't feel completely associated with either one. When I visit Italy, I no longer feel entirely Italian. I miss America and look forward to my return. When I'm back, I feel less than fully American and long to return to my Italian roots. Such is the immigrant's life.

Although I've been faced with many challenges, I've found a reservoir of inner strength to guide me through each one. This was validated for me when an elderly gentleman, learning that I was a shipwreck survivor, said, "You look like a survivor." When I asked why, he replied, "Your eyes are strong, as if they could survive anything."

In part, I attribute this to my strong faith in humanity. I learned a valuable lesson from the tragedy: when technology and Mother Nature fail us, survival is in the hands of our fellow men. It was thanks to the help and the hands of brave souls that we lived to tell our stories.

When I'm feeling reflective, I find myself filled with awe at the courage it takes to put aside self-preservation for the sake of saving others. Without a doubt, courage is the moral fiber that lets us set sail for a new dawn.

Preventing tragedies at sea must be a priority—whether facing icebergs, fog, or man-made disasters. So now I set my compass toward encouraging young people to pursue the study of marine sciences: naval architecture and engineering, oceanography, archeology, and more. A new generation of scientists will improve safety on our seas.

⁂

We gain strength, and courage, and confidence
by each experience
in which we really stop to look fear in the face. . . .
We must do that which we think we cannot.

—Eleanor Roosevelt

Album

The beautiful flagship of the Italian Line, *Andrea Doria*.

(Courtesy of Maurizio Eliseo)

Captain Piero Calamai and the *Andrea Doria's* gyrocompass,
a precise compass repeater used to establish bearings.

(Courtesy of Maurizio Eliseo)

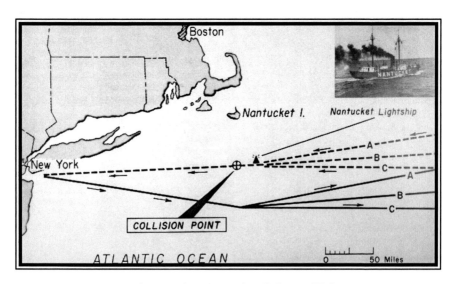

Location and approach of the collision.

(Courtesy of Maurizio Eliseo)

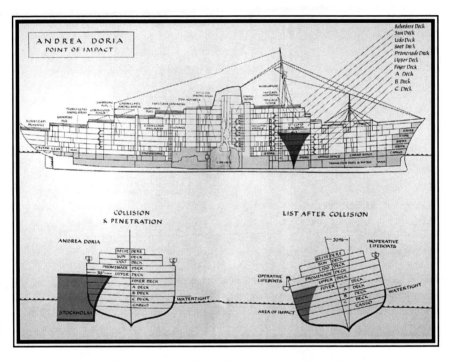

Schematic of the *Andrea Doria* and point of impact.

(Courtesy of *Saved! The Story of the Andrea Doria*)

The *Stockholm's* bow mostly missing and carrying remnants
from the *Andrea Doria*.

(Pierette Simpson personal collection)

"The *Andrea Doria* Sinks," drawing by fourth-grader Michael Azzopardi, Detroit Country Day School. He drew it two years after he heard me tell the *Andrea Doria* story.

Piera recognized herself in film footage from the *Ile de France,* which rescued passengers from the *Andrea Doria* after it was hit by the *Stockholm.*

Watercolor by James R. Gatto depicting the *Andrea Doria's* bow hitting bottom while the propeller was still above water. The wreck lies 250 feet deep.

(Courtesy of Steve Gatto)

226

Notes from the Author

I believe I survived the dreadful collision so that I could tell the real story about that mysterious night on the Atlantic.

Although I have created a work of historical fiction, the facts about the *Andrea Doria* and its last voyage are scientifically accurate. The captain and the officers are real people, and their names remain unchanged. Most characters and their stories have been fictionalized but are based on fact. One character, *Titanic* survivor Ernest Murphy, was created to honor another notable shipwreck. Through him, we learn about redemption.

For readers who are seeking factual information, both human and scientific, I refer you to my previous book, *Alive on the* Andrea Doria! *The Greatest Sea Rescue in History* (www. pierettesimpson.com). It was the basis for two documentaries: *PBS Secrets of the Dead: Andrea Doria* and, in Italy, *La Lunga Notte dell'Andrea Doria.*

For readers who wish to plunge more deeply into the human drama, I offer you this novel. While I wrote it for young adults, I hope it will appeal to readers of all ages. My main intention is to recount a fascinating historical event. If it also serves to inspire young adults to pursue the study of marine sciences, I would be pleased.

Some brief facts about the disaster:

- The *Andrea Doria–Stockholm* collision is called "the most controversial maritime event ever."

- Fatalities: 46 out of 1,706 passengers on the *Andrea Doria*, 5 on the *Stockholm*—hence the most successful maritime rescue in peacetime.

- It was the first major event covered on television in "real time." The coverage sent shockwaves around the world.

- My research, based on interviews with maritime scientists in Italy and the United States, reveals that human error on the *Stockholm* was the reason for the collision.

- The *Andrea Doria* lies in a large heap (only part of the main structure is intact) 250 feet below the ocean surface.

- The *Stockholm,* after being repaired and resold to several companies, continues to sail as a cruise ship.

- Fifteen divers have lost their lives exploring the treacherous wreck. Some of the precious artwork, china, crystal, and silver have been recovered and are exhibited in various venues. (The "Norseman" prototype car was never seen again.) A virtual tour is provided online at: http://uwex.us/Andrea%20Doria%20display.htm.

Acknowledgments and Sources

I owe my deepest gratitude to countless people: my students of all grades who planted the seed for this project, my mother for saving countless documents, *Andrea Doria* survivors who shared painful memories, and marine scientists who offered their expertise and trusted me to use it wisely.

Without the assistance of the following people, my book would not have been completed. William Garzke and Sean Kery shared their experiences of sea travel and the science of naval architecture and edited the manuscript for scientific accuracy. John Moyer provided menus, technical documents, and video footage of the *Andrea Doria*.

I also thank librarians at the Novi (Mich.) Public Library and elsewhere for their invaluable guidance, Maggie Terry for consulting, and my faithful Facebook friends Doug Kitchener, Mike Poirier, Klaus Dorneich, Sandy Roth, and others for ideas and encouragement. I'm also grateful for friends who have provided valuable advice: Katana Abbott, Elizabeth Atkins, Scott Frush, and Karlheinz Baumann. Thank you to Scott Latham and Drew Olsen, who offered story-line suggestions from a young person's point of view. I extend special thanks to Wendy Keebler for her professional editing.

My deepest thanks to Richard, who has lovingly supported all of my endeavors. You are the music in my heart that sustains the wind beneath my wings.

Sources

Scientific and human accounts for this book were drawn mainly from *Alive on the* Andrea Doria*! The Greatest Sea Rescue in History* by Pierette Domenica Simpson (Purple Mountain Press, 2006, and Morgan James, 2008); *Cento Uno Viaggi* by Maurizio Eliseo (Hoepli, 2006); *Saved! The Story of the* Andrea Doria by William Hoffer (Simon & Schuster, 1979); *Voyages: The Official Journal of the Titanic International Society;* and www.andreadoria.org.

Photographs are reproduced with permission from Maurizio Eliseo, Steve Gatto, and John Moyer.

About the Author

Pierette Simpson's first book, *Alive on the* Andrea Doria*! The Greatest Sea Rescue in History,* is the only all-inclusive shipwreck account written by a female survivor. It was published in Italy as *L'ultima notte dell'Andrea Doria.*

Ms. Simpson's book has inspired two documentaries: *PBS Secrets of the Dead*: *Andrea Doria* and, in Italy, *La Lunga Notte dell'Andrea Doria.*

The author is a member of the national marine forensics committee of the Society of Naval Architects and Marine Engineers. Her goal is to continue working with marine scientists and shipwreck divers to improve safety on our seas. Ms. Simpson also realizes her goals by telling her personal survival story to varied audiences.

In her former career, she taught foreign languages for thirty-seven years.

Ms. Simpson lives in Michigan, where she enjoys the company of her special companion, friends, family, and her two Siamese cats.

www.pierettesimpson.com

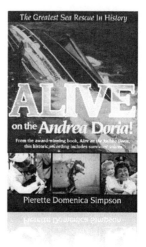

CPSIA information can be obtained at www.ICGtesting.com
Printed in the USA
BVOW071118210413

318637BV00001B/32/P